THE RIPPER FROM RAWHIDE

Fast on the grab and twice as accurate—that was Comanche John. He'd traveled a steep, far piece during his hell-roaring years of roaming and road-agenting—sleeping on the ground, dodging bullets and hangman's ropes.

Some called him the worst side-winding varmit that ever rode the outlaw trail, but John figgered it wasn't nohow wrong to rob from the rich and give to the poor.

Dan Cushman was born in Osceola, Michigan, and grew up on the Cree Indian reservation in Montana. He graduated from the University of Montana with a Bachelor of Science degree in 1934 and pursued a career in mining as a prospector, assayer, and geologist before turning to journalism. In the early 1940s his novelette-length stories began appearing regularly in such Fiction House magazines as *North-West Romances* and *Frontier Stories*. Later in the decade his North-Western and Western stories as well as fiction set in the Far East and Africa began appearing in *Action Stories, Adventure,* and *Short Stories.* A collection of some of his best North-Western and Western fiction has recently been published, *Voyageurs of the Midnight Sun* (1995), with a Foreword by John Jakes who cites Cushman as a major influence in his own work. The character Comanche John, a Montana road agent featured in numerous rollicking magazine adventures, also appears in Cushman's first novel, *Montana, Here I Be* (1950) and in two later novels. *Stay Away, Joe,* which first appeared in 1953, is an amusing novel about the mixture, and occasional collision, of Indian culture and Anglo-American culture among the Métis (French Indians) living on a reservation in Montana. The novel became a bestseller and remains a classic to this day, greatly loved especially by Indian peoples for its truthfulness and humor. Yet, while humor became Cushman's hallmark in such later novels as *The Old Copper Collar* (1957) and *Goodbye, Old Dry* (1959), he also produced significant historical fiction in *The Silver Mountain* (1957), concerned with the mining and politics of silver in Montana in the 1890s. This novel won a Gold Spur Award from the Western Writers of America. His fiction remains notable for its breadth, ranging all the way from a story of the cattle frontier in *Tall Wyoming* (1957) to a poignant and memorable portrait of small town life in Michigan just before the Great War in *The Grand and the Glorious* (1963). More recent fiction such as *Rusty Irons* (1984) combines both the humor for which he is best known and the darker hues to be found in *The Silver Mountain.* His most recent novels are *In Alaska With Shipwreck Kelly* (1995) and *Valley of the Thousand Smokes* (1996).

THE RIPPER FROM RAWHIDE

Dan Cushman

First published Laurie, 1953

This hardback edition 2000
by Chivers Press
by arrangement with
Golden West Literary Agency

ISBN 0 7540 8093 5

British Library Cataloguing in Publication Data available

Printed and bound in Great Britain by
Redwood Books, Trowbridge, Wiltshire

CHAPTER ONE

THE BLACK-WHISKERED MAN had ridden a long way. For miles he kept his gunpowder-roan pony at a weary amble, following a ridge through jack pine. Then, with evening on the way, he reined in to look down on the headwaters of the Lemhi River and the old Mormon road that was now the great highway to the bonanza camps of Montana.

He was shorter and broader than most men. His age might have been thirty-five or forty; it was hard to tell through the tangle of whiskers that covered his face. His skin, where it was visible, was brown as Spanish leather. Dusty homespun pants were thrust in the tops of his dusty jack boots. Over his linsey shirt was a vest of Nez Percé buckskin with most of the beadwork gone. Around his waist, on heavy leather belts, hung a brace of Navy Colts.

His eyes swept the road as far as it was visible, then, with his chew of tobacco rolled to one cheek, he sang in a monotone:

> "Co-man-che John is a highwayman
>   He hails from County Pike,
> And whenever he draws his Navies out
>   'Tis share and share alike;
> He takes the gold and silver,
>   He takes the greenbacks too,
> Oh, listen to my stor-ee,
>   I'll tell ye what he do:
>
> "Co-man-che rode to I-dee-ho
>   On the old Snake River trail,
> He robbed the coach at Pistol Rock
>   And stopped the Western mail—"

5

He suddenly halted. There was no sound except the faint roaring movement of evening wind currents through the evergreens; then he heard it—the distant pound and echo of gunfire.

He rode on, apparently as slouched and careless as ever, but he stayed in the timber, and his eyes missed nothing. After a mile or two the trail turned a shoulder of the ridge, and he had a view of some buildings and corrals—an abandoned freight station.

As he watched, a gun exploded from one of the cabin windows. By twilight, both flash and smoke were visible.

The bullet hit somewhere along a hillside, glanced with a screech, and two guns answered from the depths of an aspen grove. The shooting told him there was one man in the house, and perhaps seven firing at him.

The whiskered man freshened his chew. The fight in no manner concerned him, and despite its one-sided nature he had no compelling urge to participate. Making himself comfortable, with one leg crooked around the apple horn of his saddle, he went on with his song:

> "Co-man-che rode to I-dee-ho
> On the old Snake River trail,
> He robbed the coach at Pistol Rock
> And stopped the Western mail."

There were other stanzas. The song seemed endless. The fight went on as twilight settled.

Then, after minutes of silence, some of the attackers crept up and started a fire at the far end of a horse shed connected to the house. The fire spread, and for the first time the whiskered man showed concern.

"Why, that's a low Yankee trick if I ever seen one."

He decided to ride down.

It was now very dark in the timber, but he rode with the bridle slack, trusting the superior instinct of the horse.

6

Although the fire was still far from the house, the besieged man decided to make a run for it.

There was a sudden volley, then a bull-voiced man shouted: "The gully! Damn it, you let him git away. Dave, block that gully. Sellers, you watch the other side."

The whiskered man had stiffened, with his jack boots ramming the stirrups. He had recognized the voice.

"Gar Robel! Why, damn his yella bushwack hide!"

There was no doubt of his purpose now. With a hitch of his body he drew his right-hand Navy.

The gunpowder roan became skittish.

"Easy, boy," the whiskered man said. He had the kind of voice that quieted a horse.

The rough descending trail emerged from timber. Now the fight was just below. Darkness was laced by gun flame in half a dozen places.

The bull-voiced Robel kept bellowing orders to his men. "Dave, watch the up side. He'll run for it."

"We crippled him. He *can't* run."

"Well, don't let him hole up. Go in there and finish him off. Claus! Claus!"

"Here!" Claus shouted.

"Well, get over by that rock, the big one. Wolf, where are you?"

Black Whiskers dismounted and quickly looped the bridle to a pine branch. He went downhill in a series of sliding leaps, over rocks and windfalls, over slick accumulations of pine needles.

Light from the fire revealed the shadowy movements of men. They were converging on the gully.

He checked his descent. At a crouch he cut loose with both Navies, and the unexpected onslaught sent them scrambling for cover.

"Claus!" one of them shouted. "Claus, you dirty fool, it's *us*."

7

The black-whiskered man moved downward. He found cover behind crags, behind tree trunks. He bellowed:

"Claus, ye say? I'm Comanche John. Ye hear that, ye yella back shooters? This is Comanche John from the Yuba River, the man they wrote the opry about."

They responded with a volley in his direction. He descended amid flying lead, aiming back at the flame of their pistols.

"Yipee! I'm a ring-tailed ripper from the Rawhide Mountains! I was raised on corn likker and country sorghum! I sleep with my boots on, and I ain't had a bath since I swum the North Platte in the year of Forty-Nine. So crawl in your snake holes, you dirty abolitionists, because this looks like a good spot to start a cemetery."

Bullets tearing the heartwood of a tree left a burnt sawdust smell. Lead glanced off rock and roared overhead. Powdered bits of rock struck his face and left one eye momentarily blinded.

He was in the open. He kept going. A growth of juniper was both concealment and obstruction. He went through boots first. He ran, bent double, in a series of bounding leaps, and crashed into brush. He checked himself with the undercut edge of the gully beneath him.

He had left the big half-rotted windfall fifty feet uphill. Their bullets tore it to pieces. The pungent smell of wood mixed with raw powder smoke drifted past him.

He got his breath, and spat out the dirt and pine droppings that had found their way inside his mouth. He wiped sweat with the sleeve of his linsey shirt.

"Works up a man's appy-tite," he muttered.

The bull-voiced man was shouting questions.

"It's Comanche John!" the one called Sellers answered.

"You fool, Comanche John has been dead these fourmonth. They hung him in Boise City."

The black-whiskered man muttered: "They hung me

8

in Yuba, too. And in Placerville, and Oregon Bar, and in Yallerjack."

He rolled the cylinders of his Navies, and tested each chamber with the small finger of his left hand to find the empty ones. He reloaded, ramming the charges of powder and ball each with a swift series of movements so long practiced that he needed neither to see nor to grope, but moved automatically while his eyes traveled along the black-shadowed gully below.

It was an abrupt cut, ten feet deep, choked with brush. A damp smell told him there was a spring somewhere.

He finished loading, and called in a guarded voice:

"You, thar! This is Comanche John. It is, for a fact, out to do his daily deed in the cause o' righteousness."

A brittle snap of twigs answered him. He saw movement, then a man, crawling and having a hard time of it. He had a gun in one hand, and was dragging a parfleche bag that kept getting caught in the brush.

"Here I be! Up the side."

"John?"

John was surprised. "Ye know me from somewhar?"

"Pistol Rock." He spoke with effort, at the end of a grunting breath. "Remember? I was with—Whisky Anderson. Came with him—from Oregon. I was with you— at Dutchman's Bar."

"Why, dang it, yes. You're the skinny one that went by the handle of Dakotah Red. You're hit, lad."

"I tooken one in the side. I'll make it."

"Sure ye'll make it. I'm here to see that ye make it. Come a bit closer."

Comanche John lay full length, with his boots wide for leverage, and reached down with his right arm.

"Closer, lad. See if ye can stand. Reach up and get hold o' them washed-out roots. Here, hand me that parfleche bag."

9

John, reaching far down, grabbed the parfleche. The wounded man, with an unexpected show of strength, ripped it away from him.

"Leave it alone or I'll kill you!"

"Lad, don't be an idjit. I could have kilt ye already."

"You ain't fooling me! They sent you down here."

"Robel and his crowd?"

"Yes!"

"For that parfleche? What would I be wanting with that? It don't feel to have much weight of gold in 'er. Now quit raving foolish, and give me your hand."

Dakotah was slightly reassured. He breathed, and started to get to his feet. He had fallen with one leg bent under him. After repeated efforts he got to one knee, then put his gun back in its holster; but he clung fast to the parfleche. It was a skin pouch made to be carried behind a saddle, big enough to hold no more than a change or two of clothes. On its top, shining in the dim light, was a triangle and flower decoration in squaw beadwork.

It took him a few seconds to find his strength, then, with the help of the roots, he drew himself to a standing position while dirt showered over him.

"Lock wrists," John said, reaching far. "Good hold, now. Up!"

Dakotah was not a heavy man, and, rolling, John lifted him easily over the side.

"Whar ye hit?"

"I—don't know." He lay on his stomach, lips close to the earth, getting breath. "Whole side of me feels dead."

"You tooken one, all right. Here, in the side. Missed your tangled-up innards. That makes it not so bad, except for bleeding. I can't doctor ye. Not here. We'll have to git moving. Got a horse around?"

"Went lame. That's how they caught up with me."

"Gar Robel?"

"Yes."

"Why they after ye?"

"Vigilantes. That's what they call themselves."

John laughed, and called Robel a suitable name.

"After you too?" whispered Dakotah.

"No-o. Not exactly. Only, Gar and me shared the same blanket down in Californy. We did, for a fact. And when he left, he took it with him. I'd already heered how he got in with the vigilantes, down around I-dee-ho City, and was hanging his old friends. Now, lad, we better git moving. No matter what side Gar's on, he's tougher'n bull meat in Janawary. Here, get your arm across my shoulders. Better give me that parfleche—"

"No!"

The guns had been silent for ten seconds. Now Dakotah's voice brought a new volley.

John lay flat on his stomach, with bullet-cut leaves fluttering over him. When the shooting died down, he got hold of the wounded man and, half dragging him, moved back through trees and buckbrush to the hillside.

"Stay here!" he said.

He climbed alone, found the gunpowder, and led him downhill. Dakotah was on his feet, using a tree for support.

"Good lad! Now, take your time. Here, he's an Injun pony, so mount on the off side. I'll give ye a'boost. Whar they leave their horses?"

"I don't know. They came down the crick on foot."

"Can ye ride, or should I tie ye down? Here, put that gun belt over the horn. Now, listen. This pony has brains enough to play euchre with a Chinee; he has, for a fact, so give him his head, and he'll go yonder toward the Beaverhead, which is whar he come from. You let him amble. I'll pick me a steed and ride after ye."

He waited with his guns poised, ready to give him a

covering fire if need be, but the gunpowder moved away, his rawhide-covered hoofs making no sound through rock and forest cover, his black-pepper color a perfect camouflage in the shadow of the pines. Dakotah rode bent over, one hand on the horn, the other arm hugging the parfleche tight against his stomach. He was quickly lost from view. There was no new alarm.

CHAPTER TWO

"Parfleche," Comanche John muttered after long speculation. "Now I wonder. Warn't no weight o' gold in her. Greenbacks, maybe. Who'd worry that much for a packet o' greenbacks? Won't be worth two cents on the dollar when old Robbie Lee takes Washington."

He followed the hill, and made a wide circle of the burning house. He walked with long steps, but without much hurry, and he took time to freshen his chew of tobacco along the way. A winding deer trail took him to the V-shaped cut of Nephi Creek.

There was still an occasional gunshot, and Gar Robel still bellowed commands; but the distance made it seem impersonal. It was cool near the creek. The air was filled with the fragrance of horse mint.

He lay on his stomach and drank, then walked on with water dripping from his whiskers. The path opened onto a tiny meadow, and a man's alarmed voice stopped him with the word, "Hey!"

"Why, yes, lad." His voice was an easy drawl. "I'm here looking for my horse."

"Who are *you?*"

"Ye mean ye don't recognize me, your pardner good

12

and true?"

The voice was both shaky and taut: "Step out in the open."

"Why, lad, there's no need of it, because I have room to shoot ye from here."

A gun blazed from the shadow, but John, on speaking, had moved to one side. He heard the whip and twig rattle of the bullet.

He fired from a crouching position, with one hand touching the ground. He fired twice more as he moved at a weaving run. He had heard the stamp and blowing of horses, and headed toward them.

One of them broke away. The dark form loomed over him, then thundered past, kicking water and creek gravel in his face.

He was up to his knees in the stream. Water, cold as ice, shocked his feet as it filled his jack boots. He waded on, and found a horse that had lunged shoulder-deep in brush halfway up the almost perpendicular north bank of the creek.

He grabbed the bridle, but it was jerked from his fingers. He made a dive, and got hold of the saddle horn. He held on as the horse took him up to his thighs in the creek. Water slowed the animal, so that he was able to pull himself to the saddle. Leaning forward, he grabbed the reins.

He let the horse carry him, satisfied for the moment to stay in the saddle. He rode down the creek bottom at a gallop. The creek at that point was shallow and broad over a gravel bottom. A solid bower of limbs shut out the sky and threatened to tear him from the saddle. He saw the light of the burning building, and at last brought the horse around against a tight rein.

"Here, now!" he said into the horse's ear. "Here, boy. We might as well get friendly, because we'll be together all the way to Montana. Ye ever been to Montana? Heap better'n I-dee-ho, horse. It is for a fact. This is poor-scratch country compared with Montana. Why, up thar they take the coarse gold and let the fine stuff slide with the tailings. Mormon oats at fifty cents a pound, that's what I'll feed ye when we git to Montana."

His voice and his hand calmed the animal. Soon they were moving at an easy gait around the corrals and through the timber. The freight road was half a mile downstream from the burning house. They followed it. It was a fine night, cool and fragrant, with the moon just rising.

Back of him, at times, there were gunshots, but too distant for alarm. Again he sang, the words joggled out of him by the ambling rhythm of his horse:

> "Co-man-che rode to Kansas
>   With a pal named Injun Ike,
> A very shady char-ac-ter
>   Who'd broke from jail in Pike;
> But Ike got drunk in Leav-en-worth
>   And ended up in jail,
> And they led him to a hangman's rope
>   Ere John could go his bail."

He rode with long stirrups, his head back, his eyes almost closed. The night breeze dried his homespun pants, but trapped creek water still gurgled in his jack boots. He seemed to be almost asleep, but it took only a slight twitch from his horse to bring him up alert, his eyes roving the uphill shadows.

He called, "Ho, thar!"

Dakotah answered, "I'm here."

It seemed to take all his effort, and John could hear him breathing afterward.

He rode toward the sound.

Dakotah said, "I heard 'em shooting—up the crick."

"Oh, that. There *war* some lead flying around, but I met up with none of it. Didn't expect I would. I wasn't born to git shot. Nor hung, even. Got a gypsy's word for it. She told me so when I crossed her palm with gold down in Denver City. Said I was fated to die respected and full o' years, in bed, betwixt linen sheets, with my Navies hung on the bedpost, and my boots off." He groped forward as he talked, fending jack timber aside, got hold of the gunpowder's bridle, and looked into Dakotah's face. "How are ye, lad?"

"I don't know. One side of me still feels dead."

John laid his palm over the wound. Blood, drying, had stiffened the shirt, but there was slick fresh blood, too. Riding had kept the wound open. Nevertheless, they had to go on.

"Don't move more'n ye have to. Just ride. I'll take care o' the bridle."

They returned to the road. The valley narrowed and widened again, and the moon rose. The wounded man did not speak. He was bent far forward, head nodding with the movements of the horse, one hand on the saddle horn, the other arm clutching the parfleche tightly to his abdomen. He slid little by little to one side, and he would have fallen had it not been for the gun belt looped over the saddle horn.

Comanche John dismounted and snubbed Dakotah's boots to the stirrups with strips of whang leather. It took him five minutes. Afterward he listened. No shots, no voices, no sign of pursuit; just the night stillness and the wind in the trees.

He turned from the road along an almost invisible trail that took them across some flats, forded the stream, and became more plainly marked when it entered timber. It led them around sidehills, up a narrow gulch, and ended

15

at a shanty almost hidden in spruce.

Dakotah still slept. John dismounted, limping a bit from the stiffness of his legs, and spoke:

"Dakotah! Here's home for the night, lad."

The wounded man came awake with alarm that started him clawing for the Navy at his hip, and John had to wrestle with him.

"Easy, boy. Easy, now. This is your friend, the old Comanche."

"Where's the parfleche?"

"Right here. Ye haven't once let go of it."

"Where are we?" His voice, as he looked around, had a wild note.

"Shanty. Old trap-line wickiup. I just happen to know about it."

John untied Dakotah's boots from the stirrups, caught him as he fell toward the ground, and helped him inside, through the low doorway. After making him comfortable with spruce boughs heaped on an old spring-pole bunk, John started a fire with flint and steel in the rock and mud-mortar fireplace.

"How far we come?" Dakotah asked.

"Two, three hour." John spoke between puffs as he caught a spark on pitch tinder and blew it first to a spreading coal, and then to flame. "They're way yonder. Must have burnt ten pound of powder after we left. How'd they bring it along? by Conestoga wagon? If Robbie Lee had powder like that, he'd a tooken Boston already. Wish I had some whisky for ye, lad. Best I can do is chawin' tobacky."

He got the fire going, and suddenly the tiny cabin was stifling hot. He had no utensil for heating water, so he lined a hole in the earth with buckskin from his bedroll cover, filled it with water, and added stones heated in the fire. He tore a ragged linsey shirt in half, boiled it, and let half of it dry over the fire for bandage while using the other half to clean the wound.

The bullet had entered on the left side, shattered one of the lower ribs, glanced upward, and lodged somewhere deep inside the chest. Probing would have been useless.

"Can you get it?" Dakotah asked through teeth clenched against pain. He stared intensely at the smoky pole ceiling. Sweat stood in drops on his upper lip and his forehead.

"I'll not probe for it. Not now or ever. Ye gained in weight by the amount of one rifle ball. But don't let that worry ye. When I was fighting in the Kansas elections, a friend o' mine took one in the chest like, and it sickened him some, and every time the weather turned damp he'd take to bed with the horse croup; but one day, years later, I'll be hanged if he didn't cough up that bullet. Yes, he did; only nobody realized it was the bullet until his old woman cut it in half, so coated it was with the green pizens of his body. Now, lad, I'm going to cauterize the wound with a hot stone and tobacky, and it'll pain a bit."

The experience left Dakotah weak and drenched with sweat. He lay without moving while John completed the bandaging. Afterward he slept. The fire died, and the hours of night passed. When the stars commenced to gray out, John aroused him.

"Time to get going."

"Where to?" Dakotah's voice sounded better now.

"Up the trail. Over the Bitterroots. To Bannack, Alder, Last Chance, one o' them Montana camps. I-dee-ho has been a bit inhospitable toward me of late, and to tell the truth I'm none too sure o' Montana, either."

He put Dakotah on the bay horse, again cinching him to the saddle horn, snubbing his feet to the stirrups.

They reached a ridge and followed it. They followed deer trails down branching gullies until, with sunrise blinding their eyes, they came out on the wide valley of Texas Creek, which shortly joined the Lemhi.

The day grew hot. Miles away, across the bottoms, three glints of white emerged. They were the canvas tops of wagons, stampeders, probably, heading toward Bannack Pass and the Montana gold fields. Behind them there was no sign of pursuit.

John stopped at noon, shot a grouse, roasted it on a prop stick, and tried to get Dakotah to eat. He wouldn't, but he drank almost a hatful of water from the creek.

"We through the pass?"

"We got a ways to travel before we git to the pass. This is the forks of the Lemhi."

They struck the freight road, and followed it northeastward into the mountains. By late afternoon snowbanks commenced to appear, and wind with a glacial tang to it flowed down from the pass.

The freight road became a zigzag switchback hacked from a rocky ridge. It dropped over a crest, and followed the precipitous side of a gulch. Far below a stream beat itself to a white froth over boulders.

The sun set, and suddenly it was so cold that John shivered and tied the thongs of his buckskin vest. He took hold of Dakotah's arm to awaken him.

"Be ye cold?"

"I'm all right. Where are we?"

"This is Canyon Creek. The pass is yonder, still a bit of a climb. By grab, I wish I'd worn my woolen underdrawers. This mountain climate has the feel of Janawary."

He got a blanket from his bedroll, cut a slit in the middle of it, and, making a rude poncho, fitted it over Dakotah. He had just finished when the faint *click-click* of a falling stone came to his ears.

"Now, don't go to hefting your gun metal," he said,

"because chances are it ain't them. This is a popular highway. Best estimate is that ten thousand people have crossed this way in the two, three year since John White struck the bonanza color at Bannack."

They rode on through twilight, with the sun still shining on the crags a thousand feet above. The road looped inward, following a side gulch. Timber made it almost night. It cut through snow. There was a rude log bridge with a tiny creek roaring beneath. The road doubled back and kept climbing. Across and below, where shortly before they had traveled, John's roving eyes glimpsed movement.

He drew up and watched. He counted seven men on horseback. They were traveling hard. Straight across they were scarcely more than half a mile away, though by the switchback road two or three miles separated them.

"They coming?" Dakotah asked.

"Ay, lad, and so's the night."

Darkness was settling, with a wintry mist covering moon and stars. Half an hour had passed. On the wind came a tang of wood smoke. They turned a bend at one of the high levels of the pass and found the three wagons they had sighted earlier on the Lemhi.

The wagons were drawn together where the road widened briefly against a steeply plunging gully. They were freight wagons, loaded with Salt Lake flour, and not the prairie schooners of Pike's Peakers that John had surmised. The fire, half sheltered from the wind, blew bright and dim, and the shadow figures of men could be seen around it.

He stopped and called through cupped hands: "Hey, thar! Ye hear me? We be pilgrims from I-dee-ho bound for the gold fields, and mighty nigh froze for need of coffee."

There was no sign of men now. They were in the

shadows with guns ready, for the pass had long been a favorite of road agents.

"Ride into the light!" a voice said.

"Ay."

As they advanced into the firelight, a second voice said, "Why, one of 'em seems to be wounded."

John drew up where the wagons hid them from the view of anyone down the gulch. "He tooken one, that's true; but we'll not tarry for all that. Just a coffee, if ye don't mind."

A short young man, no more than twenty-one but already boasting a long silky yellow beard, walked around a wagon and got the pot off the fire, using a folded gunnysack to protect his hand. He poured the steaming liquid into two heavy metal cups, handed both cups to John, and said, "You must be in one hell of a hurry, stranger. Is somebody following you?"

John, blowing the cups alternately, said, "Why, son, this be a gold-rush year." He held one of the cups to Dakotah's lips. "And while thar's nothing we'd rather do than linger and swap yarns by the fire, I'm afeard somebody would get in ahead and stake our gravel."

A big rawboned man with a cheekful of tobacco came out and said: "You better get him inside the wagon. There'll be snow tonight, by the feel of things."

"Thank-ee, but we've vowed to cross over the pass tonight. Heered the climate was better for a man's health on the Montana side."

Dakotah had finished his coffee, and was shivering violently. He let go the saddle horn to hold the blanket poncho more closely around him.

"More?" John asked.

"I've had enough. Let's get to moving."

John drank, pausing between gulps to keep watch down the road. He finished, tossed the grounds aside, and handed the cup back.

He said, "Ah!" and tightened his belt. The heat of the coffee had left scales on his tongue, but its warmth, on a cold night, fortified his insides.

"Thank-ee," he said. "Thank-ee and farewell."

The road cleared a bulge of the mountain where the wind got a fresh sweep at them. It now carried fine hard pellets of snow. After half an hour the snow thickened. It came in flakes that weighted a man's hatbrim and formed a thick cover over the coats of the horses. The skyline was no longer visible, nor the edge of the road, nor sometimes even the ears of the horse ahead.

The bay kept balking until finally, despite the bridle, he turned around with his hindquarters to the wind and his head in the shelter of the bank.

John said: "It's no use. Some horses have more judgment than a man. Best we wait."

He sat against the bank with a saddle blanket over his head, and listened to the breathing of the wounded man beside him. He dozed and came awake many times. Snow weighted the saddle blanket and pressed it around his shoulders. His feet became paralyzed from cold, and he got up to stamp life back into them.

It was still night, but the stars were coming out, and the snow had diminished to a few listless flakes.

He awakened Dakotah and got him back on the horse. By that time a bright streak of dawn was showing in the V of the pass ahead. In an hour they reached the top. It was the Continental Divide, a high roof of the world, with the limitless miles of mountain Montana lying below, its first slopes white from new snow, and then a sea of forest, green and purple. The snow thinned and turned soggy in the sun. Little streams of water ran down the wagon ruts.

Back of them the riders again came in sight. At that

distance it was impossible to be certain, but the man in the lead seemed to have the stiff-legged, stiff-backed posture of Gar Robel.

John speeded the horses, but for half a mile he resisted the danger of a slippery downhill gallop. Suddenly a bullet struck the bank at one side. Stung by flying pebbles, the bay was off at a gallop, and John urged the gunpowder to keep pace.

Bullets chased them along a mile of twisting descent until a shoulder of rock hid them. There, a thousand feet below the summit, no snow had fallen. The hoofs left no mark.

John cried "Hi-up!" and brought both horses around. He had located a little zigzag trail up the mountain through jack timber.

They climbed for a hundred yards, and stopped. Below, through forest, galloping hoofs came close, and died away. John chuckled, gnawed off a fresh chew, and said, "Fare thee well."

Dakotah had dozed again. He pulled himself erect. "They gone?"

"Yep, and so better had we. Injun trail yonder. It'll take us to Sheebang by the back door. Ever hear of it? No? Waal, that's a mark in your favor, because in time past it's been the hangout of the unrighteous, but it'll give ye a few days to get back on your feet while Robel looks for ye around Bannack and the Beaverhead."

CHAPTER THREE

SHEEBANG CITY OCCUPIED the flank of a knoll near the outlet of a tiny mountain lake. It boasted one long log house with a hay shed and some corrals, and an assortment of dugouts and shanties. Three horses watched with heads over the top corral rail. A man stood ankle-deep near the outlet of the lake, working a gold rocker with one hand and dipping water with the other. There were no other signs of life.

Leading the way, John approached warily. When they were within a hundred yards of the house, a man stepped from the porch with a sawed-off double gun in the crook of his arm.

He was fifty, overweight but still powerful. He walked with a stooped shuffle. He wore moccasins, filthy cotton pants and a blue shirt that was held across his chest by a single button. On his head was a beaver hat that once had been a grand affair, but was now battered and slick from sweat and dirt. His hair fell to his shoulders. His face was covered by a mat of graying whiskers.

He stopped, chewed his tobacco, and spat as John came up.

"Why, it's Piegan Bill!" John said, as though he had just realized the man's identity. "I'd heered you'd got bit by your own likker and died."

"What are *you* doing, riding up here?" The voice was a husky growl across vocal cords long eroded by whisky. "You're the one that should be dead. Prospector through here in April said you'd got hung in Idaho City."

"They hung somebody, but the best information I got he was an impostor. Anyhow, it warn't me. What's wrong with ye, Bill, forgot your old friends? Have ye jined up with the law-and-order boys and took to stranglin'?"

"I jined with no law and order, but I'm not spitting in their eye, neither. I ain't puttin' up the people I did one time. Things have changed here in the Beaverhead. You know how many hangings we've had in the last twelve-month? Twenty-three, actual count, between here and

23

Alder Gulch. While we're on the subject of old friends, my advice to you is to git back to Idaho where you come from."

"Twen-tee-three!" John said, drawing out the words. "They must have been freighting in rope by the twelve-horse team. Well, times be bad all over. Did ye hear about Clubfoot Jim Hames? They hung him in Lewiston. And they cotched up with Neewah Johnny just a week later at Orofino. But that don't make much never mind to me. I've turned over a new leaf. Shacked up nearly all one winter with a sky pilot, and he gave me religion. Oh, don't narrow your eyes at me, because that's the gospel. I hit the sawdust trail. No more robbery and plunder for me. You ask me something about the Bible. Go ahead, ask it. Ask me about Moses, and I don't mean whar he was when the light went out, either."

"You got no more religion than a Boggs County hawg."

"I did, Piegan. I gave up coach robbery, and bank robbery, too. I know they been accusing me of things, but I'm innocent as a babe unborn. Share and share alike is my motto."

"Who's that with you?"

"Handle of Dakotah."

"He looks nigh dead. He's been shot. Say, are you on the lope? If you are, you can keep right on loping. I'll not have you bring the law in here on me."

"Why, he had a run in with some bushwhackers, and we headed here—the closest place." He swung down, and stamped life in his horse-stiffened legs. "I ain't the man I used to be, and that's a fact. A day or three of riding rusts all my hinges. I'm going to do like you, Piegan. I'm going to find me a good squaw and settle down."

There were other signs of life now. Most of the camp's residents were breeds and Indians. One of the breeds was Joe Bushwell, who had been chased from High Ore

Camp with a coating of tar and feathers several years earlier. A sluice robber. John pretended not to see him while helping Dakotah down from his horse.

Dakotah whispered, "Give me the parfleche."

He clung to the stirrup while John got the parfleche free of its fastenings and gave it to him. He let go and tried to walk, but his legs refused to bear him and he sat down, one foot bent under him, the other straight out. He struggled futilely to get up, but his pinned foot held him.

John said: "Here now, don't try to walk. I'll carry ye. Yes, I'll carry ye and the parfleche both. Piegan, have somebody get a bed ready."

Piegan reluctantly sent a halfbreed boy who led them down the porch and inside a dark, square little room. There was a bunk against the far wall heaped with patchwork quilts, filthy and ruptured, with chunks of cotton batt leaking out.

John saw it and bellowed. "Git that corruption out o' thar. Chop fresh spruce boughs and fetch some clean blankets. This yere lad is a friend of Comanche John, and he gits the best."

Piegan behind him growled, "You paying for all this?"

"I'll pay ye off in lead if things don't improve. Step lively, now. Send for hot water and bandage. And put the stewpot on. By grab, I'm so lank I can hear my backbone rattle every time I scratch my stomach."

An Indian girl arrived with blankets, and stood holding them in her strong arms while giving orders to the boy in the Blackfoot tongue, sending him for young spruce boughs, making him place them in the correct manner, their tip ends overlapping, their stumps on the outside so that the wounded man could roll over without being stabbed in the ribs. She was about seventeen, erect, unsmiling, but good-looking.

A fat middle-aged squaw shuffled in with a pan of hot water which she placed on the floor. John knew her to be Gopher Girl, Piegan Bill's wife.

"You go on. Get out," she said to Comanche John. "You kill him on horseback."

"I'll carry him to the bunk."

"All right, then you go away."

John deposited him in the bunk, made a sour remark, and slouched outside.

Joe Bushwell, the sluice robber, said, "You taking orders from squaws these days, Comanche?"

"I learnt years ago not to argue with women of all colors, but I take no lip from sluice robbers, because in my book a sluice robber is the next thing lower'n an abolitionist."

Comanche John found the kitchen and helped himself to the pot of venison stew. His stomach filled, he flopped down in the room next to Dakotah's, and slept. He had intended only a catnap, but he slept long. Suddenly, a noise startled him. He sat up in the bunk, a Navy in each hand. The room was quite dark. It took him a few seconds to recover his bearings. Through the door he could see a slice of meadow and mountain. It was late twilight.

He put the guns back, strapped the belts, tugged on his jack boots, and looked around for his hat before realizing he had slept in it. He heard voices again, and recognized them. They belonged to Gar Robel and his Idaho "vigilantes." He stood just outside his door, and from the next room he could hear the breathing of the wounded man. It had a rapid, irregular rhythm.

He moved over, peered into the blackness inside, and said, "Ho, thar!"

The Indian girl answered in a single syllable, "Ya."

"He wake up?"

"No. Sleep all time."

26

"Fever?"

"Plenty hot. Plenty seek."

"Clean him up? Fix poultice?"

"Ya."

"You're a good gal. You stick with him. I'll see to it you git paid. I'll buy a new red dress. I'll buy ye the reddest dress in Montana Territory."

"I stay."

"He still hanging tight to that parfleche bag?"

"All time. Pillow. You want?"

"No. And don't let anybody else take it."

He walked on, a slouching figure in the shadow of the awning. A man rode bareback up from the lake, driving horses to the corral, some of them still saddled. A candle had been lighted in the main room of the sheebang, and he heard, among others, the loud rough voice of Gar Robel.

He went inside. The room was big and low-ceilinged, half store and half saloon. Candles in a three-way holder shone down on six men with their backs toward him, drinking from chipped crockery cups while Piegan Bill stood guard over a jug.

For a few seconds John's approach went unnoticed; then the biggest of the men, Gar Robel, swung around and saw him.

Robel stopped with a backward stiffening of his massive frame. He was about six feet one, and weighed 190 pounds. He was lean and tough, without an ounce of fat on him anywhere. He was no more than thirty, although his caribou face made him seem older. He carried a gun at each hip—not the common Navy Colts, but heavy double pistols made to shoot buckshot. In an armpit holster was a Wells Fargo model Colt. In a sheath behind his right hip was a heavy old-time Green River hunting knife. The total weight of the arms he bore must have been about twenty pounds, but he carried it with indifference.

He recovered from momentary surprise and stood with his hands on his hips, grinning through clenched teeth at Comanche John. "So it *was* you!"

"It was, and it is."

Gar Robel laughed with a backward toss of his head. He decided it was even funnier. He shouted laughter, he lifted his right hand and drove the heel of it to the bar with a force that made the whisky jug do a jig and skitter to the edge, where Piegan Bill made a lunge and saved it.

"Look him over, boys, the old Comanche in person!"

John, in his slouched manner, had crossed the room. His whiskered jaw revolved around the tobacco. His black slouch hat, battered more than ever from sleeping in it, was tilted over his eyes. There were dry spruce needles from the bunk in his whiskers, and he kept scratching them out. He paid little attention to anyone, including Robel, and found a place at the bar with the wall at his back and the long room under his gaze. There he leaned aside to blast a stream of tobacco juice across the floor. He hitched his homespuns and both gun belts with his two thumbs, and spoke:

"Yep, it's me, for a fact. I come yonder by accident; and though it ain't my policy to interfere in other folks' business, seven, eight on one offends my sense of equity, especially when the strong side resorts to an Injun trick like burning a man out of a house. All of ye git away? Why, that's the worst evening I've had in years. But, as ye know, it war dark."

Robel was still smiling, but the smile had changed. His lips were pressed together, and the outside corners of his mouth were drawn down.

"You brought him here?"

"He's here, as ye know good and well. No, don't go

looking for him. Stay whar ye are. Live for a while. Save your money and put it in gold-mining shares. Marry a squaw and raise yourself a family. Dee-velop the West. You git to fooling around that lad, and you'll never again go nowhar or do nothing. Yea, verily, he'll chop ye up with buckshot until ye look like Blackfeet jerky."

Gar Robel said, "We'll get him."

"Why ye so set on it? He's away from I-dee-ho now. Whyn't ye let Montana worry? By grab, Montana's well enough supplied with road agents, so one more or less won't ever be noticed." Then he asked, "It *is* true what I heered about you taking up with the vigilantes down on Snake River?"

Gar thought for a moment. "We were friends once, John."

"We were."

"Just because I'm on the other side of the table doesn't mean we can't be friends now."

John said, "Um!" and rolled his chew of tobacco, while his gaze was long and thoughtful. "Ye seemed to have turned over a new leaf. The Gar Robel I recall liked to get his bullyrag way on everything."

"I don't turn against my old friends, and I'll not turn against my new friends either. When Briscoe was elected sheriff at Oregon Bar, he named me his chief deputy. When those diggings played out and Briscoe went back East, it was natural folks at the new Canyon Diggings would turn to me. I'm not letting them down, John. No more am I letting down my old friends from California. So don't give me that kind of an eye, and keep your hands away from your Navies. I know you can outdraw any man in the room, and maybe any two men in the room. But you count up the odds. Go ahead, count 'em up. You start trouble, John, and we'll write the last verse of that song the teamsters made up about you."

John said: "Now, I doubt it. Gypsy down in Denver City told me I was fated to die in bed, with my boots off. Now tell me why you're so set on catching up with Dakotah."

"Remember the Sipes boys who ran the ferry at the mouth of Whalen Creek? They put him up, and he ran off with $3,000 in gold. Fell in with French Pete Larue, and shot Larue while he was asleep. Unless I mistake, French Pete was a pal of yours, too."

"Dakotah is a wild one, and born to git hung maybe, but I don't think he'd shoot a man whilst he slept."

A short, dark, and very dirty man came around to Robel's right and said: "They were together, and we found French Pete in his bed, with a bullet in his back. What do you make of that?"

John said, "Maybe *you* shot him in the back."

Robel elbowed the short man away, "All right, Dave, don't start anything." Then to John, *"You're* on the wanted list down in the Snake River diggings too."

"I *am?*"

"But we might overlook it."

"Thankee."

"Provided you co-operate."

"How?"

"Now don't get that ornery look again." Robel grabbed the jug and banged it down on the bar in front of him. "Here, have a snort of this; it'll put you in a better frame of mind."

John sniffed the jug. "Frame o' mind? Stuff like this would frame a man inside a coffin. This is a concoction of the devil; it is, for a fact. Mixture of snake venom, tobacky juice and scoroflooic acid. In civilized spots like Denver City, they use this to blue the bar'ls of guns." He splashed some in a cup, and drank, all the while keeping watch. "It ain't Dakotah ye should be looking to hang. It should be Piegan thar. Honest to the Scripture. I'd rather be bit by a mad dog than that kind of likker."

"That whisky's better than the money I'm gettin'," Piegan said.

John said, "Pay the man."

Robel ignored the suggestion. He took possession of the jug and slid it back down the bar, where it again went the rounds. He rubbed a two-day bristle of whiskers on his jaw, and gave John his thoughtful scrutiny. His manner had hardened.

"I get what I go for. You know me that well, Comanche."

"What if Dakotah ain't mine to give?"

Robel's brittle temper broke, and he shouted: "We're here to get him! Get him easy if we can, or rough if we have to. Now, I've tried to be decent with you, and if—"

"Whoa, whoa! You always was the impatient one. Don't git in a lather unless ye aim to git shaved, that's my motto. Now here ye be, abusing old Comanche John, the dearest friend a vigilante ever had. Don't laugh! I'm telling ye, as sure as Providence, that my advice will save one or two amongst ye from greeting the dawn stiff and cold with four cubits of dirt on your chest. That's the gospel, boys, because he's yonder with a brace of Navies by his bed, and one eye on the door. But if ye wait—" He tapped his chest. "He was hit here. The bullet seemed to travel up, and it lodged deep. He lost blood all the way, and now he's started to fever up. I doubt he'll live tomorrow through."

Gar Robel did not believe him. He swung around and looked at Piegan Bill, who nodded in his truculent manner, and said, "My squaw says he's bad off."

"Send for her!"

When Gopher Girl shuffled in, and her husband asked her to tell how the wounded man was, she said: "Bad. Heap bad. Lose much blood. Talk crazy."

"Will he die?" Robel asked.

"Maybe, 'long about tomorrow night, him die."

"Oh," he said, apparently gratified by the news, and then to John, "But don't try anything."

CHAPTER FOUR

COMANCHE JOHN SAT OUTSIDE in the cool night with his boots off. The prospector who earlier had been operating the rocker was now sitting cross-legged in the light from the door, using a magnet to pick black sand from his gold concentrate. Inside, the jug still went around.

"How's she go to the pan?" John asked.

The man was old, and he had a whining voice. "Some days I get a quarter-ounce, and sometimes I don't even turn the color."

John, picking some strings of boiled venison from his teeth with the point of his bowie, said: "Why, that's Chinee wage. Why don't ye drift north to the Last Chance? Ten thousand gulches north o' thar, all of 'em showing the color. And more'n gold, too. I hear tell of a mountain with veins of rubies sticking out of her. That's what I got in *my* plans. Diamonds, too, maybe. I tell ye, thar's things in that north country yonder that man has never seen before this side of the delirium tremens."

The prospector said defensively: "There's gold enough here if I hit the real paystreak. Only trouble is the false bedrock, and it keeps shifting so a man never knows when he's down to the real thing. But I'll hit it."

The Indian girl came from Dakotah's room, a shadow on soft moccasins. Her buckskin gave off a smoky odor. She stopped, regarded him in her dark manner, and said:

"He sleep now. I come back after while. Yes?"

"All right, gal. You been mighty good. And I'll not forget my promise about the red dress." He watched her move from sight around the house, and asked, "Who is she?"

"Name's Mary Bird. She's Blackfoot. Not these southern Blackfeet—she's Piegan or Blood. Claims to be the daughter of a chief, but you know how Injuns are—live in a castoff teepee and eat on boiled buffalo hoofs, but once they're two sleeps away from home they claim to be chiefs with a hundred saddle horses in their string."

"How long has she been here?"

"I pay no attention to squaws. When I get my stake, it's going to be a white woman for me."

The prospector was finished with the magnet. Pouring clear water in the pan, he began to work the concentrate, tilting the pan sharply, washing garnet sand down to the lip, where he could wipe it off with his thumb until at last he had a pinch of gold dust that made a bright shine in the candlelight from the door.

John yawned, put his bowie away, and kept talking. "When you're through with this diggings, ye want to burn that old rocker and pan the ashes. I knew a fellow, a Yankee, that bought up all the old sluice boxes on the upper Yuba. Burned 'em, he did, and loaded the ashes in an old steamboat biler he brought over from the Sacramento, and ground 'em by rolling the biler back and forth with stones and quicksilver. Made himself a small fortune. Thar's gold that ye can't see, and cracks in wood that ye can't see, and the one seeks out the other. By grab, I've heered that cottonwoods growing alongside rich placer streams will gather up gold too, so sometimes it'll pay to burn 'em; but I wouldn't know for sure, never having seen it done."

A man's shadow blocked out the candlelight, and without turning John knew it was Gar Robel.

It took Robel's eyes a while to get used to the night, then he stepped out and said, "John?"

"Here I be."

"How is he?"

"Bad off, like I said."

"Where's his outfit?"

"Outfit? You saw him leave that burning shack, and how much outfit he had. Chief thing he carried off from there was an ounce of lead."

"He had a parfleche. He was carrying it behind his saddle when we saw him on the pass."

"Good eyes!"

"Where is it?"

"Ye *try* to git that away from him! He'll kill ye. By dang, he wouldn't let *me* get my hands on it, even. What's in it?"

"I told you he robbed the ferry."

"Three thousand in gold? That was your word, or somebody's word. Three thousand adds up to thirteen, fourteen pounds, or more, when you figure that Snake River gold, half silver. There was no weight like that in the parfleche. There was no gold *at all* in the parfleche. Ye can take my word on it. I've hefted so much gold I can spot a one-pound ingot inside a bale of Texas cotton."

"How about greenbacks?"

John snorted, "Wuthless Union paper! I had one o' them greenbacks once that was supposed to be worth $100. Most bee-utiful piece of paper ye ever seen. Had Gineral Winfield Scott's picture on the front of it, and percentum coupons on one end that promised to pay a man so much extra that every half-annum he could ree-tire and live on high hog and dumplings; but when I tried to cash it for gold coin those Sacramento money-changers treated me like I was white trash with the scourge. No,

Gar, I guess he wouldn't put up too much fight for a passal of greenbacks, and I doubt you'd chase him across I-dee-ho for 'em either."

Gar Robel stood with his hands on his hips, looking down on him with narrow cold eyes. He had been drinking, but he was not drunk. That would come later, and the entire settlement would be aware of the fact, but now he was holding his liquor.

"I tried to tell you this inside, and I'm telling you again now—you're wanted in Montana and Idaho both. I could send word to Bannack and Virginia and Last Chance so they'd be on the lookout for you. I *could* do that, but I haven't. I've done you a favor, and I'd like one in return."

John said, "Um?" and lifted his eyebrows.

"I want that parfleche. I want it, and everything there was in it."

"Then what?"

"I'd forget I ever saw you."

"Not about me—what about the lad yonder?"

"All I want is the parfleche bag. Montana is welcome to him."

"I'll see what I can do."

Gar Robel laughed through his strong clenched teeth, and slapped John hard on the shoulder. "Better come in and have a drink."

"In a while. It looks right now like I got a task in front o' me."

He got up, yawned and stretched, and without putting his jack boots on, walked barefoot down the porch as far as the room. He listened for the heavy breathing and heard none, but there was a movement in the bed, and the click of a gun hammer.

"It's me, lad."

"Oh."

He went in, groped his way, struck his knee on a puncheon bench, cursed, and found the edge of the bunk. "Lad, I hate to bring this up, but they're here."

"Robel and his killers?"

"The whole strangling crew. They claim ye robbed and killed down in I-dee-ho, which is things that men git hung for, and they're here fixing to tie a knot for ye in their rope—only maybe they're not, either, because I never saw a strangler that didn't want to get his hands on some swag himself. The point is, son, they're willing to let ye go providing ye give 'em that parfleche bag, together with what they expect is in it, whatever that happens to be. Now, hold on—"

"Get out of here!"

"Lad—"

"Get out of here." He struggled to prop himself up in bed. He rammed the gun forward, sinking it into Comanche John's abdomen. "Get out and stay out. You and all of 'em."

There was a crazy edge to his voice, and the Navy had a touchy trigger.

Comanche John backed away. He kept himself silhouetted against the doorway to show that his arms were wide, and that he meant no trouble.

Outside, he took a deep breath, and wiped sweat away.

CHAPTER FIVE

AN HOUR PASSED—more than an hour. It was past midnight. Inside the big room Gar Robel's vigilantes had reached a roaring stage of drunkenness.

The short dark filthy man called Black Dave hammered the butt of his Navy on the bar and shouted: "*Whoop*-a-raw! *Whoop*-a-raw! I'm meaner'n mountain lion with his ribs a-showin'. I lived with the grizzly bears, and I got the lice to prove it. Where's the likker? Piegan, bring that likker."

The jug was empty, and so was Black Dave's purse. He lifted the jug, tried to see inside it by the flame of the smoky candles, then held it overhead and caught a few last drops on his tongue.

"Piegan, I asked for likker. Hey, you dirty squawman, don't turn a deef ear to me. I'm a vigilante, d'you hear? We've left men swingin' on pine branches for less'n this. Bring me the likker."

Piegan tried to ignore him. When he could no longer do so, he said, "You'll see more likker when I see more money."

Dave stopped shouting. He leaned over and said, "Squawman, don't crowd us too far, d'you hear?"

"I'm not afraid of you!" But Piegan's eyes proved him a liar. He backed off. "You may be running things along the Snake, but—"

Black Dave hurled the jug. It missed Piegan's head by no more than four inches, and broke in big jagged fragments against the log wall.

Others commenced to shout and urge Dave on. "Tell him about all the Injuns you killed, Dave."

"Injuns ain't all I've killed. I killed Injuns, I've killed Chinee, and I've killed human beings, all three." He drew his hunting knife, lifted it high, and drove it with two hands into the bar. "Come here!"

Piegan wanted to get away, but the bar penned him in. A man named Sellers, tall, in threadbare gambler's clothes, pulled his coat aside, drew a Navy, and let it fall with a heavy clump to the bar. "Go ahead. Do what he says."

Piegan edged reluctantly along until he was opposite

Black Dave. Dave was suddenly crafty. He grinned, showing his brownish teeth, and whispered, "Come here."

"What?"

"I want to whisper something in your ear."

When Piegan bent forward a trifle, Dave seized him by his long hair, and dragged his head across the bar. Piegan flailed with arms and legs until he felt the edge of the knife against his throat. He stiffened, his eyes rolling almost out of their sockets. He didn't even breathe.

"*Whoop*-a-raw!" Dave bellowed, and gave the head an extra twist. He had Piegan gasping for breath.

The others stamped and guffawed. They offered advice. Dave was encouraged to greater efforts. With a double handhold in Piegan's long hair, he commenced jerking Bill's head up and down, driving his chin to the bar.

"What did you say the price of your likker was?"

"Let me go!" Piegan wheezed. "I'll *give* it to you."

"Now that's more like. Only say *sir*. Show some respect around here."

"Sir!" Piegan said hoarsely.

Gar Robel came through a side door, and joined in the laughter. He rocked back, his hands on his hips, with a guffaw that drowned out the others.

"Getting a shave, Bill?" he roared.

Dave said, "You're damned betcha I'll shave him."

Gar walked behind the bar, knocking things out of his way until he had found another jug. He pulled the wooden stopper, sniffed, and poured himself a big slug. He stood for a while after drinking, blowing his breath and shuddering from the punch of the alcohol. He seemed to forget Piegan Bill's predicament until he found his path partly restricted by his hindquarters.

"Let him go, Dave."

Dave did not hear him, or did not want to hear him. He had commenced to scrape the whiskers from an area of Piegan Bill's neck by pulling him back and forth across the blade.

Robel waited to be obeyed. When Dave ignored the command, Gar's face flushed, and the muscles stood out at the sides of his jaws. He went around the end of the bar at a quick pivot, came to a stop with his feet wide and set, and drove the heel of his right hand upward to Dave's jaw.

Dave had not seen the blow coming. He lost his grip on Piegan Bill's hair, and reeled with his hands tossed high. He back peddled on limber legs, instinctively trying to keep his balance. One heel caught in the pole floor, and he went down with a jolt. He caught himself on his elbows, and remained propped up, his jaw sagging, his eyes staring and out of focus.

Robel shouted, "After this when I tell you something, *do* it!"

He turned and saw Piegan Bill crouched behind the bar, with just his eyes showing.

Bill said hoarsely, "Damn him, I'll kill him," and got up with the sawed-off shotgun in his hands.

Robel pushed the barrel aside. "I asked what the row was about."

"He wouldn't pay for his likker. None of 'em paid for their likker. Asked for my money, and they all jumped on me."

"Oh." Robel growled. He stood with one elbow on the bar and watched Black Dave, groggy, get to his feet. "He didn't mean anything. He's just out for a little fun. How much do they owe?"

"Eleven dollars."

Robel drew from his hip pocket a buckskin sack with a heavy lump of gold in the bottom. He tossed it to Piegan and watched him weigh it with shaky fingers, spilling a few colors on the floor. Robel ignored the lost gold. Something else was on his mind.

"Five and an eighth," Piegan said.

"Hundred dollars even."

"Bannack gold, yes. But this ain't Bannack. This is no more'n seven hundred fine. Look at that brassy color. It's worth no more'n $70."

"Seventy, then," he said, indicating by a jerk of his head that the $30 difference was beneath his contempt. "Come to think of it, no. Maybe I won't take any of it back. It all depends. I got something to talk over with you."

Gar poured a drink and slid the jug down the bar. "Drink up, boys, it's all paid for."

Gar slapped Piegan Bill on the back. He said something in his ear, and laughed. They had a drink, then talked together privately. When it got too noisy, they walked to the short length of counter in the store end of the room, and stood there.

Comanche John, who had been slouched against one of the porch pillars, watching through the door, now lost sight of them. They had gone outside, and he could hear their boots on the gravel pathway. A few of their words came to him. He walked to the corner and listened. Their voices came again, but in lowered tones, and drowned by a fresh whoop and holler from inside. When they went inside one of the back rooms, he moved back by the door to Dakotah's room, and listened for a long time to the troubled sound of the sick man's breathing.

A glow of light appeared around the corner of the house, and with a regular movement grew brighter. It was Gopher Girl with a tin-can lantern. In her other hand she carried a bowl of yeasty-smelling poultice.

He stopped her and said, "Whar with the lantern?"

"Poultice. I fix 'em now."

"No. Light for poultice, light for bullet." He blew it

40

out. "You'll have to change it in the dark."

Muttering under her breath, she went inside. There was a long quiet while she worked.

Gar Robel then appeared down the porch. He had someone in tow. It was the Indian girl, Mary Bird. She kept pulling back, but Robel had her arm linked, and with a casual application of **power** lifted her along. He stopped her at the door to the **big** room, where, leaning close, he said something in her ear, and sniggered. A second later they went inside.

John stopped chewing. He named Robel suitably, and watched them through the door.

Robel led her to a poker table in the store end of the room and called for the jug. He poured a big cupful and tried to get her to drink it, but she kept refusing.

Gopher Girl came outside.

John asked, "How is he?"

"More bad. Tomorrow he die."

"Well, easy come, easy go; that's how it is with life in the wild Nor-west. He drew cards in a rough game, and should have known what the pay-off was when he started." He took hold of her arm as she picked up the lantern to leave. "You been top cyard, Gopher Girl, and I'll remember ye. I'll send ye a red dress from Bannack."

"Good. Red dress plenty good."

"That gal—who sent her in thar with Gar Robel?"

"No savvy."

He kept hold of her arm, and stopped her. "You savvy heap good. He left with Piegan and came back with *her*. What happened? Did Piegan sell her?"

She cried defensively: "Me old squaw. Old squaw talk-talk, young squaw don't listen. Old squaw say go 'way, too many white men around damn' sheebang. Young squaw think maybe white man plenty good. Now she got white man. Old squaw don't give a whoop, savvy?"

"I savvy you still don't like it, and neither do I."

"White man want her for wife. Maybe plenty good white man. Plenty gold, plenty horse!"

"Gar? He's got a wife in I-dee-ho, and I guess one in Californy, too. How much did Piegan get?"

"Maybe so, hundred dollar."

"Where are her people?"

"Many dead. Smallpox."

"She must have some relatives left."

"Maybe so, at Hills Divided. Uncle. My brother, you savvy?"

"What's his name?"

"Onistah. Like you say—Calf Robe."

"I suppose he's broke, without a gotch-eared horse or a breechclout to his name."

"All my people chiefs. All my people plenty horse."

CHAPTER SIX

HE ALLOWED HER TO LEAVE. Inside, the harmonica was going again. Men slapped their hands in time; there was a thud and scrape of boots.

"Squaws in the center and bucks all around!" came a nasal, braying voice. "Step lively, Gar. She's outfootin' you."

Dakotah called to him. His voice had lost its crazy edge. He sounded beat out.

John went in, groped for the edge of the bunk, and by accident touched the parfleche. He pulled his hand away.

Dakotah whispered: "Don't worry about it. I'll give it to you."

"Thanks, but right now—"

"I heard what she said."

"You mean about the gal?"

"About *me*."

"Now, lad, that's all squaw talk. You're going to ride away from here all topside on your horse. You'll—"

"I'm going out of here feet first, and we both know it."

John stood without answering, looking down on the darkness where he was. There was no use of lying. He said, "Ay."

"Take the parfleche."

John slid it from under his head and put a rolled-up quilt in its place.

"Few ounces of gold there," Dakotah whispered. "Keep it. Have a drink on me when you get to Bannack."

"I'll by-pass Bannack, if ye don't mind. Citizens of that camp make too much fuss over me. Last visit they had a reception planned, with fireworks, and it warn't even the Fourth o' July."

Dakotah seemed to sleep, but he was gathering strength for a few more words. "Keep my guns. All my stuff."

"How about your relations? I'll have a letter writ."

"No. Black sheep. No good for anybody. Better this way."

"As ye wish, lad, only sometimes mothers love the black sheep the most, and I wouldn't needs tell her—"

"No. Listen. You keep everything. Except for one thing. In there is a buckskin bag. Take that to Bonanza Gulch. Fellow there named Paddy McCormick. Give it to him. Tell him to look for more of the same on the north bank. Tell him—compliments of the man he had by the throat that night. He'll know."

John hefted the parfleche. There was little in it—a change of clothes, the lump made by a derringer, and a second lump that was probably the buckskin bag.

"This what Gar was after—the buckskin bag?"

43

"Yes. Don't let him get it. Don't let him know you gave it to Paddy. Dirty business."

"What's dirty business?"

"Everything! I never did a decent turn for anybody. I'm no good. Never been any good. Never an honest dollar. Run out of California, run out of Oregon, run out of Montana. Want to send this back where it belongs. Do a little bit to clear the books."

John said, "Ay," and listened, waiting for him to tell more about the thing that was taking him back to Bonanza.

"You know how I started out in California? I robbed my partner. Yes, I did. We had a hundred-foot share of gulch gravel at Ophir, and when he was in Nevada City for blasting powder I took the clean-up and run out. I never been any good. Came up from Malheur Lake one time, me and Cherokee Bob. Lost my horse on the Brule. Got a lift with two wagons of pilgrims heading to the Umatilla. Just poor busted-down Kansas farmers. One day, past the Grand Ronde, we robbed 'em of their mules and drove off, letting 'em sit there. And I shot a man in the back one time, in Elk City. I never been any good. They should have hung me that time they captured me at The Dalles with that German's money."

"What'd ye do in Montana, lad?"

"What did I do every place? I never been any good. Give that buckskin bag to him. Paddy McCormick. You're a straight shooter, John. You'll do that for me."

He stopped talking. He lay so still that John thought him dead. He hunted his pulse a long while before finding a flicker of life.

"Parson," John said, addressing the darkness of the room. "I wish I'd remembered the prayer ye tried to teach me. I do, for a fact, because this lad hyar does need some praying for."

With the parfleche under his arm, he walked to the door. Gopher Girl had returned, and was waiting for him. She saw the parfleche, and said, "Now you go?"

"I'll not forget your red dress. Maybe I'll git ye one with yaller trimming and a blue sash. And a hat with a plume on it, if ye'll have the breed lad saddle my gunpowder horse and lead him around the far side of the corral, all without mentioning it to the boys inside."

"Horse already saddled. Bay horse saddled, too."

"What's that?"

"Already fix 'em. Don't want red dress. You keep red dress, keep hat."

"Say, what the thunder—"

"You ride far? Many sleeps?"

"Many sleeps."

"Maybe past the Great Falls?"

"Why, that's a question. Sometimes I plan whar I'm going, but in my line it don't always pay to share my plans with others. What is it ye got on your mind?"

"You ride to Fort Benton, you keep red dress; I pay you." From beneath her blanket she drew out a tiny buckskin bag with perhaps an ounce of gold in it. "You take. Keep 'em all time, you savvy?"

"I ain't sure that I do."

"You take girl, back Fort Benton, maybe Teton River on big flats. Always big Piegan camp on Teton River. Later on maybe Piegan go north, take girl along. Back to people in the Hills Divided. You savvy?"

"Yes, I savvy." He tossed the bag with its little bullet-sized lump of dust from hand to hand, then he leaned over and slipped it back in the front of her tightly drawn blanket. "But I don't need this. I like gold, but I'd rather have it in big chunks. Nuggets, that's my meat. I'll take her, and I'll make delivery. By grab, Gopher Girl, you're top riffle. Ye are, for a fact. When I settle down, I'm going to look around and find me a Blackfoot like you. Maybe I'll even come back and git *you*."

She shook with laughter, and drew her blanket around her with an almost forgotten coquetry. "No. Already got no-good lazy white man all time drunk."

"If I want ye, Gopher Girl, I'll not let that louse-scratching husband o' yours come in my way. I'll hit him with bullet lead, and ride off with his hair on my medicine stick."

"You take girl? You take, sure enough?"

"Sure enough."

Inside, the harmonica had sounded the Virginia reel. Soon, stamping boots almost drowned it out. John sauntered to the door. A small red-faced man was bent over, the harmonica in his cupped hands, blowing it with all his power, occasionally taking it away from his lips to call the dance: "Swing your maw, and swing your paw, and swing that gal from Arkan-*saw!*"

The girl was letting Gar Robel teach her the steps. Soon she was dancing nimbly in and out of the whirl. When the red-faced man called, "Grab your partners, and polka all," there was a mix-up, and she became Fred Sellers's partner, while Robel found himself dancing with big drunken Tom Claus.

Robel stopped abruptly, backhanding Claus out of his way. He hooked his pants with his thumbs, pulling them up around his stud-horse legs. He looked around for her. The whirl in the ruddy candlelight made it hard to see. She and Sellers were at the shadowy end of the room. Finally he saw them. Sellers was a good dancer, and she an apt pupil. Already he had her executing the sprightly step with grace and confidence, and the speed of it had excited her. Her eyes were bright, her lips slightly parted. Robel's face took on a hollow look. He reached them with long strides, grabbed her by the forearm, and dragged

46

her from Sellers's arms. She fought back with a sudden strength that surprised him, twisting from his hands. She lost her balance, sprawled backward across the pole floor, rolled, and came to a crouch, ready to dart toward the side door; but Robel, moving the instant she got away, had cut off her retreat.

She stopped; her dark eyes darted around the room. She backed slowly, with Robel following her. Behind her was the short counter heaped with trade goods, and overhead, on pegs, were bridles and other pieces of horsemen's gear.

She saw a quirt and snatched it down. As Robel started to close the remaining distance, she swung the quirt, catching him across the neck.

The shock of it brought him to a stop, his hands uplifted. Then his lips peeled back, revealing his strong teeth, and he whispered, "Why, you little Injun devil!"

He took a half-step as she retreated, sliding along the counter. His hands were down. He still grinned. He feinted with his left hand, and the lash came again, cracking as it struck his cheek. He took it without a show of pain. He laughed. He laughed louder and louder, until the sound became a series of shouts. He bent forward from the waist, his big face thrust out, his hands resting on his hips.

"Look at her, boys!" he bellowed. "Look at the gal I picked. She's *my kind o' woman!*"

He took the quirt again and again. Blood ran down his left cheek, followed his jawbone, and flew in drops from his chin as he jerked his head from one side to another, and bellowed, "Harder, *harder,* you she-wolf!"

Suddenly he stopped laughing, seized the quirt, and ripped it from her fingers. He threw it behind him, and grabbed her by both wrists. She fought him, but her strength was nothing compared to his. He forced her back against the counter, released one of her arms, and then, in a sharp maneuver, spun her around and bent her other arm in a hammerlock. He moved her arm up, little by little, between her shoulders. Pain brought a cry from her lips, and caused her knees to buckle.

"You're my gal, you understand?" He whispered, but it was a raw whisper heard throughout the room. "I paid six, seven ounces of gold for you. And I'm boss. Me. *You* say it. Say who's boss. Say who."

Comanche John came inside the door. Men fell away to both sides, clearing the way, but he did not cross the room.

He stood there, chewing slowly. His eyes were bare slits in his mahogany-brown face. His hands dangled long beneath the butts of his Navy Colts.

"Drop her, Gar!"

Robel did not hear him. He breathed heavily, and bent her arm a trifle more.

John bellowed: "Drop her!"

Then Robel heard him. Though he looked around and saw Comanche John, he did not let go of the girl. While his right hand still held her, his left sneaked for one of the double-barreled pistols.

Comanche John's response seemed casual. He made no sharp movement. There was merely a dip of his right shoulder, and the Navy was in his hand. Powder flame knifed upward through the ruddy half-light, and the room rocked with concussion.

The slug hit Robel in the forearm, which was bent at a high angle above Mary Bird's head. It struck like a sledge, carrying the arm in a helpless arc, spinning the big man with it. Robel almost fell, but saved himself on one knee. He was bullet shocked for a second or two. His staring eyes were on his shattered arm, and on the blood that ran inside his sleeve and dripped from the ends of his fingers. He recovered his faculties suddenly, and lunged to his feet. He started to draw with his good hand, but checked himself. His eyes were on the upward-tilted muzzle of Comanche John's Navy.

"Good idee," John said, his whiskers parting in a grin. "You go for that, and it'd leave me with no choice except to put these buckos of yours to the backbreak of burying your bullet-riddled carcass."

The girl was on her feet, clutching her twisted right shoulder, for the moment unable to understand what had happened.

"Gal," John said, "git over here, behind me."

Instead, she fled through the side door.

Robel shouted, "If you think you can get away with—"

"What I *think* has never been halfway so important as what I *do*."

He felt behind him with one jack boot after another, finding his way across the ax-hewn poles that formed the floor. He kept his head tilted back, and his eyes were no more on Robel than on everyone else.

"Sellers," he said, "you stay clear o' the bar. All of ye, right whar ye were." He was now framed by the door. He stopped. "And a word o' warning: first one through this door after I go out is likely to git hit with bullet lead, because I've plumb sickened o' your company."

CHAPTER SEVEN

OUTSIDE, HE TOOK A DEEP BREATH of the cool night air, and pulled the parfleche from under the bench where he had hidden it. He ran the length of the porch, stopping just beyond the corner.

"Gal!" he called. "Gal, whar be ye?"

There was no answer. Inside, everyone was shouting at once. The light went out, and he could no longer see the doorway. He fired the Navy twice in its general direction to discourage pursuit, and started toward the corral.

"Gopher Girl!" he bellowed.

He had to keep going. The moon, at that moment hidden by clouds, favored him. Robel's men were outside, but they had not seen him.

It was a hundred yards to the shed. He had covered half the distance when Tom Claus sang out, "Thar he goes!" and cut loose with his pistols.

A bullet whipped the air overhead. A second lashed stinging fragments of dirt around his legs.

Over his shoulder he glimpsed the flashes. He checked the impulse to fire back, knowing that the flame of his gun would only mark his position to the others.

Claus shouted: "Dave! Dave, you get around on the up-hill side and cut him off."

Dave answered, "Thanks, but how about *you* cuttin' him off?"

"Ya yella belly! You talk big gunfight, but you're yella belly!"

Robel was outside, cursing all of them. He began to call his men by name, telling each where to place himself.

John was now at the shed. He stopped amid the warm horse and manure smells. It was too dark to see anything. At his left, horses, spooked by the gunfire, were moving uneasily around the corral.

"Boy!" he called. "Where are ye with that gunpowder broncho, boy?"

There was a movement at the far end of the shed. He hurried toward it. It was Gopher Girl, pulling an unwilling Mary Bird along behind her.

John said, "What's wrong now, she want to stay?"

"She think all white men no good. You too."

"Why, she's close to being kee-rect on that one, she is, sure enough." He spoke to her: "Mary, ye don't need to worry about old Comanche John, because he never struck a woman yet, except in self-defense. I'm taking ye back to the Teton, plenty north, plenty sleeps, Blackfeet camp. You savvy?"

"Me savvy!" she whispered, looking at him with her wide dark eyes.

He asked Gopher Girl, "Whar be the horses?"

"Back of corral. You come. I show—"

"No, Gopher Gal, here is whar we part. You git to cover and stay thar, because in two shakes or less this shed will be buzzing like a hive full of red-hot hornets."

With Mary by the arm, he ran to the far end of the shed, to the corral.

"Through here," he said. "No, not over the top. Too good a target."

The girl slid between the quaking asp corral poles like a shadow, but it took some grunting and maneuvering for John to get his own close-coupled body through. The horses, frightened, were running. John held the Indian girl close to the corral wall to keep from being trampled.

She said: "These not our horse! Our horse outside."

"Sure, gal, and these horses will be outside too, when we're through with 'em. Whar's the gate?"

She led him to it. He had trouble moving the wooden pin that fastened it. With the gate open, he went back, bellowing, "Hi-ya!" and waving his hat and the parfleche. The stock made one more thundering circle, found the gate open, and stampeded into the night.

He followed through the dust of their flying hoofs, and found Mary Bird already mounted on the bay. The frightened halfbreed boy crouched in the poor protection of the corral, holding to the bridle reins of the gunpowder.

"Thank-ee, lad, and if any man asks whar I headed, tell him Californy by the way o' Canady, because I'm a man that hankers to git around and see the world."

He mounted with the parfleche squeezed between his waist and the saddle horn, and they were off at a gallop, chased by a scattering of long-range bullets.

A ridge hid them, and John eased off, saying: "Gar will want his arm bandaged, and it'll take 'em an hour or three to catch those spooked-up horses. And Montana, thanks to glory, is mighty big."

The trail led downhill, in and out of timber, and through the swampy backwater of beaver ponds where mosquitoes rose in swarms to meet them. For miles they followed a narrowing gulch. Dawn was coming. The mountains fell away, and they were in a country of yellow hills and scraggly timber, with the valley of the Beaverhead in the far, smoky distance.

The girl then broke a silence of hours to say, "Bannack?"

"It's yonder, off the larboard bow." He spat to indicate the direction. "That's steamboat talk, child. Laws, nobody ever came from Pike County that wasn't full up and spoutin' with steamboat talk. But we ain't going thar. Not to Bannack."

"You say you buy me red dress in Bannack."

"Now, I did, didn't I? I did promise ye such, all the while forgetting another article made o' fibre which they got stocked in abundance: to wit, rope. Anyhow, the red dresses in that town o' Bannack aren't fitten for a pretty gal like you, Mary. I'd ruther not git one in Virginny City, even. I'd ruther go clear to Bonanza Gulch, the same being the Paris of the gold fields, and not too bothered with law and order."

"You 'fraid you get hung?"

"No-o. Gypsy in Denver City made quite a pint o' the fact that I'm not *ever* going to git hung. Why, you wouldn't believe it, but when you look at me you're looking at a man that's fated to die in bed with his boots off, wealthy and respected, a country squire sort of, maybe even a congressman to the Confederate States of America."

"No savvy."

He went on talking, eyes almost closed, shaded by the black slouch hat.

"By grab, it war enough to make a body's mouth water, the way she told about it, me passing to my ree-ward like that. I can just see me now. Thar I'll be in my shiny black coffin, in store clothes, with my hands on my chest and a Navy in each one of 'em."

"Piegan say you no-good road agent."

"One o' these times, child, we'll find some beeswax to put in your ears, and then I'll tell ye just exactly what I think o' Piegan Bill. Me a road agent! Me that shacked up all one winter with a sky pilot! Why, child, it's not road agentry when ye take from the rich and give to the poor." He rubbed his pockets, and looked far off, and muttered to himself, "And right now I'm mighty poor."

The morning sun climbed, and its rays reflected hotly from the rocky ground. The bay had developed a limp that became more pronounced. John dismounted and examined the hoof. The nails of the left hind shoe had been driven too shallowly, and the hoof wall had split. He managed to pull the loose nails without getting his head kicked off, and, with that done, sat down to rest and look inside the parfleche.

It contained the usual assortment of extra clothes, a double derringer pistol of .44 caliber, a quantity of bullet lead, a packet of papers and letters ragged from long carrying, a miniature crayon portrait of a young woman. In a money belt with its buckle broken he found a small packet of gold dust, light in color and worth no more than $10 an ounce. He hefted it, appraised the weight at three ounces, and put it in his pocket.

He sat with the buckskin bag in his hand, scratched his whiskers, and muttered: "Now what would be in this? O' course, it's none o' my business what he's delivering to that Paddy McCormick, but . . ."

He opened it. The bag contained a piece of porous, whitish rock about the size of his fist. He turned the bag inside out. Nothing else. He examined the rock for a sign of some metallic mineral. There was none.

He said: "Why, this is just plain old dumpite. Not a color. Not even any pyrite o' poverty. What would Paddy McCormick be wanting with *this?*"

"No savvy," Mary Bird said.

"Me no savvy, either, child. And furthermore, what would Gar Robel be wanting with it? Why'd a man like Robel chase it all the way across I-dee-ho?"

He shrugged, and repacked the parfleche.

They rode on, hunting for the easiest going to favor the bay horse.

The season was only late May, but the sun had the intensity of August. It had been dry on that slope of the divide. The grass was poor and brownish. There were deerflies already, and with no breeze the same flies pestered the horses for miles. He watched for grouse, or any game that could be stick-roasted over a fire, but miners and hungry Indians had plucked the country clean.

He said: "You don't chaw tobacky, gal? No, and I wouldn't be the one to teach ye the habit. I seen women addicted to it, and it's not a fair sight, them around the kitchen, messing with the cooking, spitting at the ash hopper all at the same time. But tobacky *is* a comfort when a man is on wolf rations. I tell ye what, we'll ride yonder to that silver camp o' Belden. Know the storekeeper thar. Name o' Sampson. Pike County Sampson. Third or fourth cousin o' mine. Everybody from Pike County is a cousin of everybody else's. Just like Blackfeet."

A wagon road crossed the hills, and they followed it up a dusty gulch to Belden. By then it was late afternoon. Belden consisted of fifteen or twenty shanties, a burned-out saloon with only the wall logs left, and a store. Farther along were some sheds and a clay-brick charcoal smelter big enough to take ton or half-ton charges of oxidized silver ores from the mines whose pinkish dumps could be seen a quarter-mile up the slope. Now, however, the smelter was cold. In the gulch bottom four men were thumping away with a hand mortar while two others turned the crank of an amalgamation drum.

He bought provisions, and again rode south, at twilight reaching a Bannack Indian camp near Beaverhead River.

There were four teepees, patched and repatched. A smell of smoked and drying fish was everywhere. Only squaws, old men, and children were around, all the young bucks having traveled eastward toward the Three Forks in search of game.

They were welcomed, and in the morning, with the bay limping badly, they reached the blacksmith shop at Independence Rock on the Beaverhead.

The freight road was an empty ribbon of white winding westward toward Bannack, and eastward toward Virginia City and Bonanza Gulch. Smoke drifted from the stone chimney of the shop, and there was an occasional *clang! clang!* of a hammer. Downstream, in a little grassy flat, two emigrant wagons were camped peacefully, with ragged wash fluttering from a line.

"Men no come?" Mary asked.

"Robel? He'll quit when he's dead."

The blacksmith mended the bay's hoof, and took a small nugget in payment, biting it and trying it on the blackened metal of his forge before putting it in his pants pocket.

"Friend o' mine might o' passed hyar," John said. "A great joker he be, always telling folks I'm a road agent. He'd carry his arm in a sling, having broke it while doing a polka dance. Maybe five, six men with him. It'd be worth another nugget just like the one I gave ye to find out when they passed and whar they were headed."

"I never saw him! I just mind my own business."

"We stay here?" Mary asked when John came from the blacksmith shop, leading the horse.

"Sorry, gal. Better to drift on."

"Maybe Robel he cross over Beaverhead already?"

"I reckon. Probably last night. In that case, we're behind 'em, and they'll be stirring up the vigilantes all the way from hyar to Last Chance."

CHAPTER EIGHT

THEY FORDED THE BEAVERHEAD, then rode across vast flats toward the Ruby Range, its colors rust and violet in the sunset. After some miles the road forked, with one set of ruts going straight on toward Alder Gulch, and the other swinging northeastward toward the camp of Bonanza. They made the turn toward Bonanza. Far away hung the dust cloud of a wagon train.

The dust cloud faded with twilight, and it was an hour past dark when they came on the outfit, twenty-odd schooners and supply wagons pulled up in a rough circle between the cutbank walls of a coulee. In the middle of the circle a fire had burned down to a ruddy spread of coals. Candles had been lighted inside some of the cloth-covered wagons.

John reined in and sat with one leg crooked around the horn.

"Pike's Peakers!" he said, without trying to hide his contempt. "Begging your pardon, gal, but I'd say a Pike's Peaker wasn't much better'n an Injun."

He waited, and watched shadow movements around the fire. A man sawed a fiddle and sang sadly:

"The roof was tumbling inward,
    And bluebells grew over the side,
  While the mockingbird warbled so sweetly,
    'Twas the house where the o-o-old folks died."

Comanche John dried a tear that had mingled with his whiskers. "By grab, that was purty, even if he is a Pike's Peaker."

He told her not to follow, and rode, alone, into the fire-light.

"Ahoy, thar! I'm just a pilgrim out o' the night."

He ignored a couple of rifle barrels and rode directly to the fiddler, a spindly old man with a neck like a plucked rooster's.

"Be ye the one that sang that song?"

"I be."

"Wall, by grab, I've heered singing in San Francisco, and I've heered it in Saint Joe, and I've heered it in Hannibal, and that singing of yours just laid it over any I ever *did* hear. Do ye happen to know the hymn they wrote about Comanche John, that pore, martyred traveler that was hung by the neck in I-dee-ho City, heaven rest his soul?"

Flattered by the whiskered man's words, the old man tucked his fiddle under his chin again, played it and sang:

57

The Ripper from Rawhide

"Oh, gather round ye teamster men,
  And listen to my tale
Of the worst side-windin' varmint
  That rides the outlaw trail.
He wears the name Comanche John
  And he comes from old Missou,
Where many a Concord coach he stopped
  And many a gun he drew.

"He first rode down to Yuba town,
  In the good year fifty-two,
With a pal named—"

A woman shouted, "Stop it! Stop it, blast your hide!"
She charged down from one of the wagons, saving her calico dress from the cactus with one hand and holding an old-time horse pistol in the other.

She was tall and rawboned. Her hair was red, somewhat bleached by the sun, and edged with gray. She had a long face and a heavy jaw, and she had seen better days, but for all that she was not ill favored—not by the standard of most wagon women.

She stopped. "Glass!" she bellowed, addressing the fiddler, who blinked and quailed in front of her. "If I told you once, I told you a hundred times I wouldn't stand for those sinful words being howled in this camp."

"It wasn't anything. Only a song—"

"Only a song, he says." She turned to the camp and to heaven for judgment. *"Only* a song! Well, I'll tell you about *that* song, it glorifies the wicked and the sinful paths they trod."

Comanche John had retreated. He half turned, got rid of his chew of tobacco, then stood with his hands folded corpselike over his chest and his eyes rolled heavenward.

He said, "I pre-ceeve that you're a Christian woman, ma'am, and begging your pardon—"

"Who are *you?*"

"Me?"

"I ain't talkin' to President Lincoln!"

John thought it over while she observed him without charity. He needed his chew, but it was gone. He tried to speak. He swallowed, and tried to speak again.

She shouted: "Why don't you say something? Has whisky burnt off your tongue?"

"Whisky, ma'am? I beg ye not to utter that fearful word in my presence. Not to *me,* a man that signed the pledge on the bloody plains of Kansas in the year of Fifty-three!"

"Well, maybe," she said, somewhat mollified, "but you have the watery-eyed look of a whisky drinker to me."

"They're tears, ma'am, tears of gladness that I'd had the good fate to fall in with religious folk, for I am a stranger amongst ye, heavy-laden and sore pressed; and that's straight from the Psalms of David, it is for a certainty."

"You're mighty heavy-laden with Sam Colt metal, I'll say that for you."

"I wouldn't be, ma'am, except for the wickedness of this world, and that I'd heered it bruited on the best authority that thar be them tha'd do me bodily harm."

"What's your name?"

John took time to roll an imaginary chew of tobacco and wipe his whiskers with the back of his hand.

She shouted, "What's so hard about *that* question?"

"Ma'am, I been kicked around and buffeted by Fate. I been pursued and named names that no Christian man would repeat. I have, for a fact. I had so much trial and tribulation that sometimes I forget what my real name is."

A little red-speckled, weasel-quick man who had crept up from the shadow of a wagon with a rifle in his hands said in a high, nasal voice: "I'll tell you why he don't come up with his name, Prudence. It's because—"

"Don't you call me Prudence!"

"Mrs. Browers, I mean."

"Well?"

"Because it's *him*. Look at the whiskers. And that horse. That's what's called a gunpowder roan in this country. He's the one they were talking about. He's Comanche John!" And he aimed the gun.

John stood for a time, recovering from shock and turning his black slouch hat around and around in his hands. "May I bring up the pint that the real and genuine Comanche John, him who believed in share and share alike, is right at this moment deep in his grave, having been hung by that sinful vigilance committee at I-dee-ho City?"

"I heered they'd hung him in Yellowjack."

"Yes, ma'am."

"*Both* places?"

"Then all the more reason—"

"Well, *I* say a man that's so shifty they hang him twice is likely not to git hung at all."

The freckled man cried, "O' course he's Comanche John. And there's a reward for him. Two hundred ounces in Bannack gold! You know how much that'd be in real money?"

The big woman growled, "No."

"Right near $3,500!"

"Blood money!" she said, under her breath.

"What?"

She shouted in exasperation: "Listen here, Spotsy Huss, I'll not filthy my hands with blood money. It's un-Christian."

"Then I'll take it and give you the glory of ridding the territory of a killing road agent." Spotsy kept the rifle pointed. "Anyhow, it ought to be mine, most of it. It was me that recognized him."

John tried not to look at the gun, or to be shaken by the fact that it was cocked, and that the little man, in his nervousness, gripped it too tightly; but Spotsy stayed on the move, little by little, keeping John in the clear. By firelight, the knuckles of his hands looked like china, and the rifle muzzle, because of his tenseness, kept trembling. John killed time by gnawing off a cheekful of tobacco. He hooked his cartridge belts where they crossed, lifting them a notch around his abdomen.

Spotsy cried: "Don't try anything! I warn you, that's dead-or-alive money, and I'll shoot!"

John kept his hands innocent. He spat at the fire, then drawled: "Now, that'd be too bad for both of us if ye shot. You'd show up with the wrong body, and like as not ye'd git hung for the mistake. So let's talk this over like Christian human beings. Did I hear you rightly that somebody war here looking for Comanche John?"

"Yes."

"Who were they?"

"Vigilantes."

"In this country we generally call 'em stranglers."

"They represented the law!"

"What variety? I-dee-ho law, or Montana?"

"Both."

John stood a trifle straighter. "How many?"

"Twelve, thirteen."

"Twelve," a teamster said.

"And I suppose the one leading 'em was a big scoundrel with his right arm in a sling?"

Spotsy nodded.

The crowd had gathered tightly around to listen, and now a bull-voiced man was trying to bellow his way through.

"Make room, make room!" He was head and shoulders over most of the others. "Move aside, you hide wallopers.

Who's captain around here?"

Spotsy waved him away. "Don't get in front of me."

The big man burst through, and came to a stop with his startled eyes on the rifle. He puffed and blew. He had the build of an ox. He stood with his boots set wide and his head and shoulders thrust forward. He had a sawed-off shotgun in one hand, and carried a coiled bull whip in the other. His hat, beard, and rough clothing were powdered by the fine whitish dust of the Beaverhead.

"Hey?"

"We got him. This is Comanche John!"

"So it's *you!*" he said to John.

"And who be you?"

"I'm the captain here. Browers."

The blacksmith on Beaverhead had mentioned him. "Buffalo Browers?"

"I been called that."

"Waal, I been called Smith."

Spotsy cried: "He's Comanche John, the same one the reward was up for at the express office in Bannack. Two hundred ounces of gold. I guess that'd help this wagon train along quite a considerable, two hundred ounces of gold!"

"Blood money!" said Prudence.

"It's *money*," growled Buffalo Browers.

"Well, I don't like it! I don't like anything about it. Look at that arm-slung vigilante that rode up here saying do this, do that, all high and mighty. Wanted to search my wagon. I'll see him hung on his own rope before he pokes his nose in *my* wagon."

"Oh, that's damn' foolishness. Got to kill off the road agents like they kill off the wolves, or it ain't safe for any of us; and if there's some easy gold dust in it, why—"

"It's not Christian, Mr. Browers."

"Amen!" said Comanche John.

Buffalo bellowed: "Woman, your place is back inside the wagon. Go look after your chores."

"No." She stood her ground. "Mr. Browers, it's a man's business to pint his nose toward hell, but it's woman's business to save him from going there. That's the vow I took when I married ye in the town of Independence. I vowed to save your immortal soul whether ye liked it or not, and I'll not be swayed."

"You mean you'll give shelter to road agents?"

"No, I mean I'll find out which one's the biggest varmint, this black-whiskered one or him with his arm in the sling."

The old fiddler quavered, "I don't see how this pilgrim could be Comanche John if they already hung him twice," and in the background several of the teamsters laughed.

"We didn't ask for your shilling's worth," Buffalo said.

The big man kept stamping around so that Spotsy had to make room.

"Keep clear of my gun!" he wailed.

Spotsy retreated until he was almost in the fire. It scorched his hocks, and he jumped. For an instant the gun was no longer leveled. John, with a quick reach, seized the barrel and lifted it overhead. The gun exploded, and bullet and flame whipped upward through the night. It was a single-shot gun, but Spotsy still fought for it. John let him have it, and spilled him backward. He lay sprawled on the ground, blinking into the muzzle of John's right-hand Navy.

John held the Navy and looked around.

"Know what Comanche John—the *real* Comanche John —would have done right then? Why, he'd have had his man for supper, he would, for a fact. And then he'd have lit out on his horse and got away. But I ain't done any of those things." He let the words sink in, then he lowered the Navy and put it back in its holster. He stood with his hands spread out. "Ye see, them with righteousness has got nothing to fear, not even in the wild Nor'west."

"Amen!" said Prudence. "We should hang our heads in shame."

John went on: "Now I'll give ye the facts. That arm-slung vigilante, Gar Robel, ain't so much looking for *me*, or for Comanche John, may he rest in peace, but for a gal. Yes, he is. He's searching for a gal. A child, really. A poor, motherless child that he bought with gold from a renegade in Sheebang City." He addressed Prudence Browers, "A saloon owner, that's what he bought her from! A saloon owner that had her prisoner, chained to the wall in his den of rum and iniquity, trying to learn her the liquor habit; but thanks be to Providence, I happened to chance along, and rescued her. I did, for a fact, and I brought her here by day and by night, ducking the bullets of the unrighteous."

"Listen to that lie!" Buffalo said.

"Think so, do ye?" And John, cupping his hands, shouted into the brush shadow above the creek: "Mary! Mary Bird, be ye thar? It's all safe. These be Christian folk."

There was an answering crack of twigs, and Mary Bird rode into sight, letting the horse pick a crooked trail down the bank, across the creek, and into the firelight as emigrant men, women, and children parted to make room.

"Why, she's a squaw," Buffalo said with disappointment.

Prudence shouted, "A squaw! She's one o' the Lord's creeturs!"

"Debatable point."

Prudence ignored him. She threw her horse pistol to one side, and rushed with her arms outstretched.

"It's true. The stranger was telling true. She's only a

child. Just a poor, motherless child. You come on down here, now. Come on. I 'low you do looked peaked. When's the last you had something to eat?" She looked around and saw her husband. "Don't just stand there with your face hanging down like a coon dog's. Go git the stewpan on."

She helped Mary Bird down from her horse, and felt her over for broken bones.

"Let me once get my hands on that wicked saloon-keeper. Let me only one time."

"Much hungry," said Mary Bird.

"He's telling the truth, ain't he?" She pointed to Comanche John.

"Sure. We ride away at night. Ride away much fast. *Bang, bang.* Very bad."

"You poor child. You poor, motherless child!"

CHAPTER NINE

SEATED AGAINST THE HIGH REAR WHEEL of the Browers's old Conestoga wagon, Comanche John ate vension stew, stabbing huge pieces of meat and whole dumplings, and carrying them inside his mouth on the point of his bowie. He had a refill, mopped up the last succulent drop of gravy on a biscuit, and was left with just strength enough to unbuckle his belt before collapsing with his back against the wheel. There, his hands folded across his stomach, he said:

"By dang, I swore to get hitched to a Blackfeet squaw when it came my time in life to settle down, but grub like that is enough to change my mind. I tell ye, I've et beef stew in Taos, and I've fed on high hog and dumpling in

Pike County, Missouri, and I've had buffaler stew on the Platte, but this stew of Prudence Browers just lays it over any stew I ever did have."

Prudence, from the rear door of the wagon, said, "I 'low I've saved my last heel of maple sugar for the past five hundred mile, and tomorrow I'm going to cook you one of my special dried apple pies."

"Why, thank-ee. That'd be Christian of ye."

Buffalo Browers, a massive, truculent shadow, looked down on him from over her shoulder.

"Tell me this: How come Robel could get the Bannack vigilantes to riding with him if there's no more'n a runaway Injun girl at stake?"

"Ain't ye heered that when the devil calls there's always the legions of hell that answers?"

"Amen!" said Prudence. "When I hear you speaking truths like that, I can't understand how I ever came to mistake you for that varmint Comanche John."

"May he rest in peace."

"A-amen!"

He digested venison stew as Prudence fixed a bed for Mary Bird inside the wagon. The camp grew quiet, as the fire died to a dull red beneath a coating of ash. A lone man on sentry duty rode in a slow circle around the cutbank rims, but little danger existed there, far from the Blackfoot country.

At last John got up. He yawned, stretched himself, and looked around for a likely place to sleep.

The creek brush was deep, dense, and inviting. He started over, and found the old fiddler waiting for him between two of the wagons.

"*I* don't think Comanche John is so much a varmint," he whispered in gleeful secrecy. "And they ain't fooling me when they say they hung him over in I-dee-ho City, neither."

John gave him a narrow scrutiny. "And what *do* ye think?"

"Don't take offense now, but when you said 'share and share alike,' I *knowed*. Yep, I knowed you was the real Comanche John as sure as Judgment."

"How about the ree-ward? Wouldn't ye like to collect that?"

"Not for two hundred, not for five hundred ounces! It'd take more'n that to make Ev Glass do the squeak on Comanche John! I won't whisper a word. Not on the man I think is the whooping-est, shooting-est, ring-tailed ripper that ever—"

"Now, not so loud." But John was pleased. He dug deep in his homespuns for a nugget. "Here. You take this and buy a new harmonica when ye get to Bonanza."

"Not me! I'll buy whisky." He said it in whispered defiance at Prudence Browers's wagon. "Yes, I will. And I'd rather be hung than ever git whar I'll be ordered around by a woman again. I'll buy whisky, and drink it, and blow my breath over all of 'em."

"You reckon Buffalo would sneak around and turn me over to them stranglers?"

"Not Buffalo. He'll do what Prudence tells him. Everybody in this outfit'll do what she says. Ever see her when she gets crossed? But I'll buy likker in Bonanza no matter *what* she says!"

John slept deep in the brush, with his head on the parfleche. The camp awoke him at dawn. He sat up and scratched twigs from his whiskers. It was still very early, with light on the low surrounding hills, but heavy shadow in the bottoms.

A gangling kid rode past, bareback, driving some hobbled horses. The breeze carried to his nostrils the smell of frying salt pork. He got a move on him then, ate breakfast at the endgate of Prudence Browers's wagon, and saddled the gunpowder.

Mary Bird was ready to come with him, but he said, "You stay thar. I'm going no place."

"Don't forget red dress."

"I won't."

He rode miles ahead of the wagon train, and from a rock promontory looked at the freight road for more miles ahead. Here and there were wagons and dust clouds, the usual traffic of the gold fields. At hot noon the wagon train overtook him, and he rode in the seat beside Ev Glass, the fiddler.

Glass hailed from Kansas by way of Arkansas, and was secretly but bitterly pro-Confederate. Through long hours in the battered old wagon, Comanche John found no single point of disagreement with him.

When he tired of talking, Ev sawed at the fiddle, and sang:

> "Oh, gather round ye teamster men
>   And listen to my tale
> Of the worst side-windin' varmint
>   That rides the outlaw trail.
> He wears the name Comanche John,
>   And he hails from old Missou,
> Where many a Concord coach he stopped,
>   And many a gun he drew.
>
> "He had four boon companions
>   All loyal and all true,
> They were two-gun Bob and Dillon
>   Big Dave and Henry Drew;
> They robbed the bank, they robbed the coach
>   They stopped the Union mail,
> And many a cheek did blanch to hear
>   Their names spoke on the trail."

The road unwound, hot and white and dusty, over the little hills. The Ruby Range fell away at their right, but ahead were higher mountains, belted by clouds, with snow on their summits. The pace, always slow, decreased to a crawl, with wagons spread across to grassland to let the hungry stock graze.

Comanche John chuckled, spat across the rumps of Ev's team, and said: "This outfit's in no hurry. Ain't they worried somebody else will get their gravel staked?"

"I don't guess most of the boys are fooling themselves on that score. More interested in farming than placer gravel. With spuds at six, eight dollar a hundred—"

Buffalo Browers rode up, bareback, on a big gray workhorse, and called, "You ever been over this road to Bonanza before?"

"B' night and b' day," said John.

"How long to Bonanza?"

"Three days, by Shawvigan Pass. That's the cutoff."

He guided them through foothills and mountains. The road was a steep, twisting way through a rock and forest wilderness. The second night, at six thousand feet, was so cold a crust of ice froze over the water barrels, and everyone slept under winter quilts. The country was covered by a dense mist when they arose and drove over the summit. Then the sun broke through and revealed vast slopes, heavily forested, descending toward some river bottoms.

Comanche John, after scouting ahead, returned and rode beside Browers's wagon, which Prudence was driving.

"That's the Crowfoot River," he said. "Bonanza's thar. Look close and ye can see the smoke. Over one flank of the ridge and then another. It seems close, but it's a distance. The Three Forks of the Missouri are yonder, over the mountains. Virginny City is over the mountains thar, and yonder is the Pipestone Diggings, and way farther, way, way yonder, are Last Chance, Confederate Gulch, and Eldorado." He added, with a touch of pride, "I been in all them places."

"But this road will fetch us?"

"To Bonanza, yes, ma'am."

"Why, ye been kind, and ye done us a service. But for a man of your temperament, I'd guess these old Conestogas went pretty slow."

John sensed that something was wrong. He kept the gunpowder at a slow jog beside the wagon seat, waiting for her to go on.

She said very casually, "I see that Spotsy has Nelly driving his outfit today."

"Spotsy ain't been around?"

"Not since breakfast. Come to think of it, I don't recollect seeing him even then."

"Probably rode for a stray."

"Like enough."

John had heard no talk of missing stock, and a man doesn't go off looking through a strange country on his lonesome. He pulled off the trail and waited. Sure enough, Spotsy's little beaten-down-looking wife was driving his Conestoga. John doffed his hat, wanting to speak to her, but she was obviously scared of him, and he let her go by without a word. He waited until the entire train had passed, then he rode forward to Ev Glass's wagon. Fastening the gunpowder to the endgate, he crawled forward over heaped cargo to the seat.

"You seen Spotsy?"

Ev, his mouth filled with cold buffalo jerky, shook his head.

"You suppose Spotsy would have the nerve to go it alone for that ree-ward money?"

The jerky, though boiled most of the night before, was still stringy-tough as wet gunnysack, but after several minutes Ev got it down so that he could speak.

"I 'low you don't have to worry about that Spotsy Huss, not after the fright you tossed into him that first night."

While eating jerky, Comanche John had a look at his two Navies, making sure of powder and ball, sure that each cap was in place, even checking his patent powder dispenser and pouch of bullets.

He said, "Two hundred ounces of Bannack gold is a mighty big ree-ward."

"I reckon Spotsy wouldn't think it as big as a half-ounce of Comanche John lead."

Ev giggled, and repeated the remark while getting out his fiddle. With the violin in his lap, he tuned up his vocal cords, then sang "The Night Fair Charlotte Froze to Death," "The Drunkard's Child," and "A Handful of Earth from Mother's Grave." The wagon climbed over rocks. It creaked and clumped, and jolted a man until his innards ached. Sometimes the road would be level, across pine needles as soft as a featherbed, but always after such places it would come to an abrupt downward pitch where the handbrake was necessary.

John drove so that Ev could go on fiddling and singing. Suddenly, at a blind turn through timber, they began a descent, but found that the wagon up front had stopped and was blocking the way. The lead team came to a stop, with heads up against the wagon's endgate. The wheelers tried to stop also, but no one was on the brake, and the wagon overran them. With a frightened lunge they began to climb the leaders. It was the start of a first-class tangle, and Ev, cursing, had time only to toss the fiddle inside and go for the brake.

"John!" he called, "John, where are you?"

But John was not in sight.

He got the reins, and gee-hawed the teams off on the uphill side.

Bill Harum's wagon was in front, and he could see Billy

looking around to see how he was making out.

"This is a tarnation of a place to hang me up."

"Don't blame me. We're all stopped."

"I'll lay gold to greenbacks it's that old wheel-sprung Pittsburg of Crossman's. He should have left that wagon behind at the Platte. By grab, give me a broadax and a mouthful of nails, and I'd build me a better wagon than that out of green cottonwood."

Riders crashed timber. The realization that they weren't men of the wagon train alarmed Ev.

He turned and whispered into the shadowy depths of the wagon behind him, "John!"

"Here I be."

"There's—"

"I see 'em."

"Who—"

"You mind your horses and mind your tongue. If they ask anything, you play deef and dumb."

Ev looked sick and scared. He was greenish under his tan, like a man who has just swallowed his chew of tobacco.

The horsemen were above, visible now through the jack timber. There were two of them in sight, but more were around. One of them was Black Dave. They had trouble picking a course down across slab rock and deadwood. The man with Dave was lean and hawk-faced, a stranger.

"This is it!" the hawk-faced man said, motioning to Ev's wagon.

Dave had a sawed-off shotgun in his hands. As he approached the wagon, he got down behind the neck and shoulders of his horse, with only one leg, one arm, and the brim of his hat showing.

The hawk-faced man called to the fiddler, "Your name Glass?"

72

Ev tried to answer, but he was too scared. His mouth opened, and his lips moved soundlessly. Sweat ran from under his battered old hat and mingled with his gray whiskers. He tried a second time, and his voice came in a thin pipe of sound like that of a cockerel on his first crow.

"Yes, I'm Ev Glass."

"Where is he?"

"Who?"

"You know plenty well *who*. Where's Comanche John?"

"I don't know."

The hawk-faced man drew a pistol and leveled it across his saddle horn.

"How would you like to have your head blown off?"

Ev indicated the interior of the wagon behind him. "He's there."

"Where?"

"Inside."

Dave shouted downhill through a cupped hand, "Gar! Gar, we located him."

Riders were coming around the wagons. Robel was one of them. He rode stiff-backed and stiff-legged, one arm in a sling, a double pistol in his good hand. He kept spurring his horse, trying to force the animal to a gallop against the steep and narrow limits of the trail. Wagons and teams crowded him. Branches tore at him, and he fended them off with his pistol and his good arm.

He bawled, "Where are y'u?"

"Here!" Dave answered.

Billy Harum's team was causing trouble, the leaders trying to get clear. They were off the trail uphill, giving Robel no room to pass. Robel beat at them with his pistol. Harum cursed him, and Robel cursed him back.

"By the Gawd," Robel shouted, "you raise your lip against me, and you'll swing from a pine branch beside

73

him. It's hanging in this territory to give shelter to a road agent. Where is he?"

"I don't know what you're talking about."

"I'm talking about Comanche John."

"Haven't seen him."

Dave called: "Here! Gar, here. We got him cornered."

"Where?"

"Some place under the wagon sheets."

Robel, getting clear of Harum's team amid the blocky granite of the mountainside, suddenly realized that he might be the first one shot. He twisted his horse around and came to a slip-sliding halt against the wagon.

"Well, what are you waiting for?"

"There's only two of us. Get some of the boys here."

"Smoke him out!"

Dave, still bent around in the protection of his horse, shouted: "John, we know you're in the wagon. Come out with your hands up."

At his first warning of danger, Comanche John had crawled over Ev's cluttered supplies to the rear of the wagon. The gunpowder was tied there on a lead string. He got hold of the string, but he was suspicious of an ambush gun in the timber below the trail, and did not show himself. Hunkered, with only his hand and arm in view, he waited, hearing the excited voices of Ev and Harum, then the crash of horses through the dry branches above.

He unfastened the lead string, pulled the canvas wagon cover up from the box, and maneuvered the horse around so that he would not be visible from the uphill side. With his bowie he slit the canvas. He could now see without being seen. The lower side of the trail seemed safe enough, but still he waited, knowing that Gar Robel was no fool. He knew, too, Gar would have the obvious escape routes covered. John wanted to learn the positions of his pursuers before making a ride for it.

He heard Gar shouting, and drew his right-hand Navy. He remained crouched on the side of the wagon box, his left hand holding the canvas slightly open. Men were coming up through the timber below. With the noise and shouting on the other side, it was hard to judge their exact positions or their distance away. He heard Gar tell Black Dave to smoke him out, and Dave when he shouted, "John . . . come out with your hands up."

"I'll fetch him!" cried the hawk-faced one.

A pistol shot broke the mountain air. Lead whipped the wagon, passed through, and rattled in the trees beyond. A second shot, aimed lower, buried itself in Ev's bedroll, raising a smell of mildewed quilts.

"You let him get away!" Robel bellowed.

"He's hid thar," said Black Dave. "This'll fetch him!"

A charge from the shotgun tore through, and John jumped out, boots first. Riders were coming up through timber. He saw them as he leaped. He expected to be met by gunfire, and he let his legs buckle. He twisted over, catlike, close to the ground, releasing the lead rope for an instant, retrieving it, coming to a crouch, the rope in his left hand, the pistol still in his right.

John's sudden appearance caught the first of the riders coming through the timber off guard. He was a young, good-looking fellow, with a sawed-off shotgun across his pommel, but he kept it there while his eyes stared into the muzzle of the Navy six.

"Be ye looking for someone?" John asked softly.

The man opened his mouth to answer, but no sound came.

"Now that's smart of ye. Nary a word."

"Where's Stevens?" the hawk-faced man asked.

Gar Robel called, "Steve!"

The young horseman, blocked from the view of the

others by the wagon, neither glanced around nor answered. He looked as if he were ready to buckle in the middle and fall off his horse.

John whispered, "Answer him."

"Yeah?" Stevens called.

"See anything?" Robel asked.

John said, "Tell him I got away."

Stevens, with an effort, complied. "He got away."

Comanche John reached a jack boot to the stirrup. Robel was bellowing profanity, calling his men to ride the timber. Suddenly brave with the thought that John was no longer in the wagon, Black Dave rode around the endgate and caught sight of the gunpowder.

At first Dave tried to get away. Then, realizing he didn't have time, he tried to bring his sawed-off shotgun into play. He stood in the stirrups and twisted his body, with the sawed-off in both hands, but a slug from Comanche John's Navy unseated him. The sawed-off blasted wildly, and Dave was knocked over the cantle of the saddle. He fell back, his boots still in the stirrups, his elbows resting near the hips of his lunging horse. He rode for a couple of jumps, bullet shocked and helpless. The shotgun slipped from his hands, and the horse kicked it clattering over the stones. He fell, spread-eagled on his back, while his horse swapped ends and bucked over him.

The horse bucked straight down the trail toward Robel and the hawk-faced man. There was no room for him to pass, so he swapped ends again and tore uphill through the timber.

Stevens was calling: "Gar! Gar, pin him down. He's around your side!"

But Gar and the hawk-faced man were unable to do anything because of the bucking horse.

John got around the next wagon uphill. It was Solly Brown's, and he could hear the bawling of kids inside.

He cursed, but kept clear of the wagon, not wanting to draw their fire toward it. It left him no choice but to show himself. He drew his other Navy.

Then Prudence Browers's voice came to him:

"Thar's kids in them wagons, you hear me? You shoot into them wagons and, s' help me, I'll hit you with buckshot out o' this horse pistol. There'll be pieces of vigilante scattered from here to the Bannack pass."

Comanche John was up the trail at a gallop. The trail ahead of him was blocked by teams and wagons. Steep rocks lay to his right, and downward to his left, the timber. He cut over sharply, downhill, between two wagons. He was turned back by a whistling volley of gunfire.

He dived from the saddle. He was on one knee, safe for the instant, protected by a hump in the trail. Leading the gunpowder, he tried to get downhill. Stevens and his partner were ready for him. A bullet stung the earth, driving powdered rock into his face. It blinded him. He stayed down, trying to control the rearing horse that was dragging him. Finally the animal quieted. John came to a crouch and exchanged a volley. Stevens was hit and knocked down. The bullet had struck him somewhere in the leg, but he managed, with a hobble and dive, to get in the protection of the wagon wheels.

Others were on their way. John crossed to the uphill side of the trail. Again a volley greeted him.

"Why, it's e-lection day in Pike County, Missouri!"

He made a quick loop in the lead rope and got it around his arm. He was on one knee, with a Navy in each hand.

"So ye got me," he bellowed. "So ye got me cornered, now what ye going to do with me? Will ye be shot in front or arrears?"

He glimpsed movement beneath Ev's wagon. It was the hawk-faced man, trying to creep up for a potshot, but a bullet from John's left-hand Navy sent him scrambling for cover.

John whooped: "Stand in line, gents, thar's enough for one and all. Just step up and take your turn." Someone fired on him from the timber. The slug made a ticking sound close to his black slouch hat. He shot back with a Navy levelled across his thigh, but the man was already belly down, taking no chances.

"Yipee! I got cemeteries named after me all the way from Last Chance to Yuba Gulch, so give me room, because I'm Comanche John, the man they wrote the opry about."

Again the voice of Prudence Browers came to him: "Up the trail, you idiot. Ride for it!"

A charge of buckshot tore along the trail, cutting a shower of pine needles that rattled off trees and rocks.

It was Prudence Browers, with her horse pistol.

"'T' horse, t' horse, ye idiot! Ye think I can keep 'em down till suppertime?"

John shouted, "The gal—Mary Bird—"

"No harm'll come to *her,* I'll promise that!"

He swung to the saddle. The horse, badly spooked, tried to run, but was checked by the tangle of trees and deadwood bordering the trail. John kept going, forcing a way through. Wild bullets chased him. He rode blindly, bent over the neck of the horse, arms folded across his eyes for protection against the wire-hard lower branches.

There was an opening. He sat upright, and got his hat back on so that he could see. He had reached a narrow game trail. He still could not see forty feet ahead or behind. Men were shouting. They seemed to be all around him. A wild shot rattled off high and far to his right.

"Easy, boy. Easy." He talked to the gunpowder. "We been shot at before, and we'll live to be shot at again. Just so we don't break a leg on the slippery going."

The game trail was a series of level stretches broken by

steep descents. He stayed with it for a quarter-mile, then left it and climbed, crossing the road that had been traveled by the wagon train earlier that morning, and kept climbing until the timber grew scrubby, and finally petered out altogether against the talus slopes of the high ridge.

He had time to listen. Pursuit was far away. He reloaded, traveling as the horse wanted to travel, at an amble, and sang:

> "Co-man-che John is a highwayman,
>   He hails from County Pike,
> And whenever he draws his Navies out
>   'Tis share and share alike."

CHAPTER TEN

HE STOPPED WELL BEFORE SUNDOWN, grazed the horse on a rich stand of mountain grass, shot and cooked a grouse for supper. He noticed that a tie string of the parfleche was loose. He looked inside, and found that the rock was still safe. He held it at arm's length and turned it slowly.

"No gold," he muttered. "No sulphide. Not even a chloride stain. Just plain, wuthless dumpite."

What was it that Dakotah had said? Deliver it to Paddy McCormick, and tell him to look for more of the same along the north bank, with the "compliments of the man who had you by the throat."

He grunted, shrugged, and put the rock back. Dakotah had taken a hard one, and it had addled his brains. Most men would have thrown the rock away, but John had given his word, and the word of Comanche John was never given lightly. His song said so.

He slept and rode on, taking his easy time of it, and at evening he sat looking down on the camp of Bonanza. It lay in the bottom of a gulch, far below, marked by a winding sprinkle of lights. Through the cool quiet he could hear wagons, voices, the slam of doors, even the singing of a fiddle in a polka air. The music made him move restlessly and tap the instep of one jack boot against the stirrup in rhythm.

"By grab," he said to the silent trees around him, "what I need is a taste of city life."

He rode down a switchback trail that became a road, cautiously taking his time, allowing deeper darkness to settle between the steep walls of the gulch.

Bonanza was a first-class camp. From over lesser roofs, he admired the opera house. It was a square stone building, fully three stories high, with a dome, and room inside, so he'd heard, for three hundred people. He could pick out other fine structures, too—the Gold and Silver Hotel, the Bonanza House, where Bob Wilkerson had lost the $60,000 pot to Slim Jim, the gambler from Torrence. And he could see the squatty stone jail with the big bull pine behind it where they'd hung Wild Bill Finch. He had been a ring-tailed ripper, Wild Bill, quick with a gun and long on a horse, but with a failing for women and polka music, and that's how they'd found him, with his arm around a redhead and his pockets weighted with Wells Fargo gold.

Comanche John heaved a sigh for Wild Bill, and eased back still more on the gunpowder. He reached the outskirt cabins at a wary amble.

With all the flat ground of the lower Crowfoot Valley three miles away for the taking, Bonanza had chosen a gulch whose bottom scarce allowed room for the creek and the freight road. Here and there a narrow building was built at street level, but most of the structures, even the opera house, were perched on the sides, reached by stairways on trestles, stairways cut from stone, stairways and walks swung from cables.

He passed among cabins and wickiups, and later through the claptrap houses of Chinatown. The street was crowded and barely ten feet wide. He dismounted and led the gunpowder to a livery-and-feed stable, where he ordered Mormon oats for his horse at $1 a quart.

"This be a high-priced camp, sonny," he said to the big-eared, freckled boy who fetched them.

"It is lately, since the big strike at the Mexico."

"Hardrock?"

"Yep. They struck her on the ninety-foot level. Two feet of ruby silver, solid mighty near. Now they're all sinking—the Midas, the Horn Silver, the Agnes, all of 'em. You wait, this camp'll be bigger than the Comstock."

"You acquainted here?"

"*Should* be. I lived here almost a year."

"Do ye know Paddy McCormick?"

"I know *Billy* McCormick."

A gangling man, obviously his father, came from the stable to ask John if he meant Paddy McCormick, the discoverer of the Dublin Bar. "He's dead," the man said. "Robbed and murdered by the old River Gang under Comanche John when he tried to ship half a million in dust down the Yellowstone a summer ago."

"Under *Comanche John?*"

"That's what I understood. The killin' varmint. I wish I had him in *my* gunsights. Just once I wish I had him."

John grumbled, "These are mighty measly oats to what my horse is used to getting. Wormy. Full o' chaff."

"They're the best oats in the Territory!"

John went on grumbling, "*Union* Territory, Union

guv'nor, Yankees. By grab, you mark my words, there'll be a change in things when old Robbie Lee takes Washington. And I got mighty lean measure, too, if ye want my estimate."

"Rusty, run and fetch another half-measure of oats." He gave John a closer scrutiny. "And here's some friendly advice: you hadn't better make that Confederate talk too loud in this camp. There's sentiment here for hanging rebs just like road agents. By the way, haven't I seen you around some place? In Copperapolis, maybe, or in Last Chance?"

"I'm from a heap futher than Last Chance."

"I never forget a face. You give me time, and I'll remember yours."

John slid his hat a trifle farther over his eyes, and hitched his gun belts. Then he chuckled and said: "Reckon in my case ye better put it that ye never forget a whisker. Why, I wager I wouldn't know this here face myself, because I ain't shaved it in many a year. Vow I took not to shave until slavery was extended to the free and equal State o' Kansas." He addressed the boy, "Who be this *Billy* McCormick?"

His father answered: "Nephew of Paddy's, but Paddy must roll over in his grave at thought of the wastrel that's become of him. Him singing every night like a common low-down actor in that Silver Dike Saloon."

John pressed a nugget into the boy's hand and asked for directions to the Silver Dike. It was pointed out to him, high on the opposite gulch side. He rode on, up a steep road. He dismounted in the dark rear area of a saloon, tied the horse, and went on afoot, with the buckskin bag containing the white bit of rock thrust in his hip pocket.

The sights and sounds of the camp stirred him, and put an extra spring in his shuffle. Bonanza had grown since he'd seen it last. A jam-packed mass of teams and wagons were in flux along the main street. After a day of rain, the earth had been turned into a gritty quagmire. A stream, high from melting snows of the more remote peaks, flowed thick yellow in a ditch along one side. In some places there was room along the sides for a pole sidewalk, but through most of the distance the walk had been pushed up the walls of the gulch, and supported by pole trestles, giving the pedestrian a vantage point from which he could, if he chose, spit in the wagon boxes of the freighters below. Sometimes a store or saloon would be so situated that its doors opened directly onto the main walk; but most of them had constructed private stairways, and the more enterprising had placed barkers at the turn-offs to bring their attractions to the attention of the passer-by.

"New York Dance Hall," said the man in the checkered vest. "How about it, Whiskers? Dance with the most beautiful girl in the territory for $1, only the fourteenth part of an ounce of gold."

Comanche John was tempted, but he remembered Wild Bill Finch, and walked on.

"High Riffle Saloon, genuine Saint Louis beer."

The man looked at no one; he merely chanted, and kept pointing with his cane.

"Honest Solomon's for pants, coats, boots. Please take the card. Every Saturday night the lucky number wins free pants."

"Why, thank-ee," said John.

"Out of the way, Abe, can't you see that the whiskered gent already has pants? Well, you'll laugh the pair you got right off yourself at the free show, the same show that played for two hundred consecutive nights at the Bar Royal in the city of San Francisco."

"I'll be back."

"Bed for the night, $5. Bed for the night . . ."

"Not yet, thank-ee."

"Hey you, hey you! This is the stairway to wealth and fortune. The High Riffle Palace of Chance, sky's the limit, miner. Come in with an ounce and go home with a million. Only a fool works for a living. . . ."

"Why, them's my sentiments, too."

"Please, look at tintype picture of Chinese girl? Chinese girl very beautiful."

"Why, ye-es. O' course, I was always partial to Blackfeet gals, myself. Sa-ay, this *is* a gal, ain't it? Hold on, I ain't finished looking—"

"So sowwy, please. You climb steps see beautiful Chinese girl much better as picture."

John kept going along the crazy walks and streets of the boom camp. He stopped suddenly when he saw a tall gaunt man sitting cross-legged on a barrel, strumming a banjo.

"Why, damme, it's White Eyes!"

The man was blind, and his hearing was more acute because of his blindness. He heard the voice, and recognition brought him up with his spine stiff as a rifle barrel. His eyes were milk-white, and they stared at the night sky above Comanche John's head. He started to speak, checked himself, and instead strummed the banjo vigorously while he sang in a husky but strangely musical voice:

> "Oh, gather round ye teamster men
>   And listen unto me,
> Whilst I sing of old Comanche John
>   The fastest gun thar be.
> I'll tell of how he robbed the bank,
>   And how he stopped the mail,
> And how he locked the sheriff
>   In the Eldorado jail.

"Now, Co-man-che rode to Beaverhead
In the merry month of May
With a hundred thousand in his purse,
And—"

"It warn't May," John said, moving close. "It war in December, and it war thirty degrees below zero, and I war bankrupt except for a Mexican dollar, a side o' salt pork, and five gallon of trade likker." He kept hold of White Eyes's right hand to stop him from playing, and into the other pressed a nugget. "Thar. That's a bit for ye. It ain't up to my usual style, but I been seeing hard times lately, riding the straight and bankrupt, having hit the sawdust trail and given up stage robbery for nigh onto a twelve-month, except for one measly Wells Fargo mudwagon just for old time's sake."

"But you come!" White Eyes whispered. "It's what I said, that it'd be mighty like for the old Comanche to come ridin' in here, right into camp, just to spit in their eyes."

"No-o, I quieted down some. I have, for a fact. From here on it's me for the peaceful life. I'm heading north, White Eyes. I'm going to find me a Blackfeet squaw and settle down."

"*Comanche John* settle down? When that day comes, I'll burn my banjo and move in with the Chinee. I'll do worse'n that—I'll jine the Yankees."

"No, White Eyes. Thar comes a time in every man's life, and I come to that time in mine."

White Eyes slid down on the barrel. He poked the air around him with the neck of his banjo to make certain that no one except John was close, then he spoke in a whisper from behind his hand:

"They're after ye, John. Oh, I been listening. My hearing is better'n most men's. It is, ever since I lost the sight

85

of my eyes in the Sacramento fire of Fifty-one. And I heered things. The town is crawling with vigilantes like lice on a grizzly. Robel, do ye remember him? Yes, the same Robel that was run out of Yuba, down in Californy, after he killed those two Jenkins boys. Turned vigilante now, and—"

"I know all about him. So he's in town." John chuckled, "But do they know *I'm* in town?"

"They know, I reckon. Something about an Injun gal. I heered things, but I haven't quite pieced them together. You keep away from that Injun gal, because the second you go close to her they'll ambush you."

"I wouldn't like that," said John. He looked around with his mouth sour at the corners. "This camp ain't my style nohow. I never did like a gulch camp so steep a man couldn't navigate it with a horse. B'sides, this end of the Territory's too filled up and settled for my nature. Getting so a man can't ride for twenty-four hours without sighting the smoke of a cabin, and I'm one that craves elbow room. Canady, now *thar's* the place! Trees that reach for ten thousand mile, and nary a rope on one of 'em." He felt the piece of rock in his pocket. "But first I'm looking for young Billy McCormick. Is he yonder at the Silver Dike?"

White Eyes held up his hand for quiet. A tenor voice floated down to them, pure and musical, above other voices. "Listen! That's him, singing that low-down Irish song. If there's one thing I can't abide, it's a young, able-bodied man, like him, going around singing, taking customers away from the blind." He asked hopefully, "Be ye come here to shoot him?"

"Why, I'd like, just to favor ye, I would for a fact." Clapping White Eyes on the shoulder, John walked on, guided uphill by the clear tenor of Billy McCormick's voice.

A stairway, half of wood and half cut in stone, led to the third bench level, where four dance-hall saloons stood in a row. In front of the second one, two camphine lights burned brightly in reflector brackets, illuminating a sign that read, *Silver Dike Saloon and Polka Palace.* He was close enough to understand the words of the song:

"When I was a young lad
    Upon my mither's knee,
 She called me in the shanty house
    And said these words to me:

" 'Now, when you've whiskers on your chin
    And reach a man's estate,
 You'll be obliged to toil each day,
    And never turn up late,

" 'And if you take to roaming
    In seasons wet or dry,
 You'll have to earn your livelihood
    Or fall in the gulch and die.' "

John crowded inside. He could see the singer on a little stage between a harpist and a melodeon player. He was a fine Irish specimen, tall, wide-shouldered, with a way of holding his head high. He was in his early twenties, black-haired, white-skinned, and handsome.

"Oh, when me pockets jingle,
    I dine on lager beer,
 I'm a ramblin wretch from Erin's sod
    The son of a gambol-eer."

His strong sense of rhythm carried the crowd along with him, and they stamped their boots, raising the dust of dried mud from the floor as he concluded:

"The son of a, son of a, son of a,
　　Son of a, son of a gambol-eer!"

Nuggets sailed through the smoky lamplit room and landed on the stage. Billy McCormick did not hesitate to pick them up. After accumulating all the gold he could hold in his hands, he announced that he was buying drinks, and there was a general movement toward the bar.

John, edging along, half carried by the crowd, got beside him and said, "Lad, ye hold onto that money and invest it in good sound Confederate bonds, that's my advice to you."

Billy laughed with a backward toss of his head. "What good is gold but to spend, in this Territory, where every gulch is plated with it six inches thick?" Then, seriously, "One of these times I'll settle down and start saving my money; I'll do that." And with another swift change of mood: "Sure, but you're right. What would my poor dead uncle think of me, singing for bits of gold in a saloon, him that made a million and was robbed and died from the river pirate's bullet he took on the Yellowstone?"

John kept hold of his arm, then took the buckskin bag with its fragment of whitish rock from his pocket, and pressed it in his hand.

"I was asked to deliver this to your uncle, but it will have to be you."

"What is it?"

"I was hoping you could tell me."

Standing against the press of men, Billy McCormick loosened the drawstring and shook out the rock. He looked at it by the smoky half-light.

"I know nothing of these things. Is it an ore?"

"I doubt it. To be truthful with ye, I doubt that it's anything."

"You're playing a trick on me."

"No, lad. A dying man asked me to deliver it. A dying man whose only name was Dakotah; a road agent, and bad as the worst, but with some good in him at the end. He asked me to bring it here, to Paddy McCormick, with the word that he was to look for more of the same along the north bank, compliments of the man who had him by the throat that night. Those were his words, lad." John repeated them. "And if they mean nothing to you, don't ask, because they mean nothing to me, either."

"He was drunk?"

"He was dying."

"Heaven rest his soul." He looked up from the stone. "And I am grateful to you for bringing it. Tell me, have I not seen your face somewhere?"

"Aye, I've been up one trail and down another for a year or three, and that's the truth. And here's a piece of friendly advice: Put that rock in your pocket, and say nothing, especially to a big lobo with his arm in a sling, because I wouldn't want ye to end up dead like Dakotah. Good singers are harder come by than road agents, in Montana Territory, and that's by a certainty."

Over strange voices Comanche John heard the tone of a voice familiar to him. It spelled danger. He let go of Billy McCormick's arm, and the crowd carried them apart. Billy was saying, "Wait, hold on!" but John did not stop. He reached an archway, crossed a little theater crowded with chairs and tables, found a back hall, a door, and the good cool air of the mountains beyond. He was outside, with the rear wall of the building on one side and the steep gulch on the other. He followed a path to some steps made of flattened logs set in dirt and stone.

The familiar voice was raised again. "He was here, I tell you! I'd know him any place."

The voice belonged to the little weasel-faced wagoner, Spotsy Huss.

Boots thudded along the walk. Running boots.

John did not seem to hurry, but he did not delay. He emerged into the light of saloon and stone fronts, and followed the main walk, thick with the passing crowd. There was no sound of pursuit now. White Eyes, on his barrel, without an audience, was singing "The Charge of Skelly's Brigade." John went by without speaking.

A Chinese, falling in step, said: "Please, look at picture? China girl v'y beautiful. China girl—"

John left the walk for the steep gulch side. He slid, digging his bootheels to check his descent, then reached the roadway. He worked his way among mule strings and loaded wagons. Returning to his horse from an unexpected direction, he stopped in the shadow, and waited. The gunpowder was resigned, switching at gnats, waiting. All seemed safe enough, until a man moved only a half-dozen steps away. The man was crouched on one knee, his back toward him. A bluish shine of gun metal came from his hand. He was waiting for John, with a drawn Navy.

"I should kill ye," John said quietly.

The man started around and stopped. It was the hawk-faced one. He stood holding his breath, every muscle in his body rigid.

"Yes, I should. I should kill ye. And I would, except for the noise it'd make. So I'll save ye for another time. I'll put ye down amongst my good resolutions."

The man breathed.

John said: "Drop your gun. Thar. Now unbuckle your belts. Push 'em back with your foot. Why, these are fine guns. Worth upwards of $80 each. A man never knows when he might need a couple of extra guns. Especially now Sam Colt is dead, and in his grave, up in Connecticut. The *one* Yankee in Christendom I'd give a plugged Spanish dollar for, and him dead. By grab, what's the world a-coming to?"

He looped the gun belts over the saddle horn, untied the gunpowder, and mounted.

"Now, I'm riding off mighty slow, taking my time. Make your move whenever ye like, but if you're still in the range of my Navies it'll be your *last* move."

He rode down to the street, and out of sight beyond log buildings. He passed the livery stable and Chinatown. The buildings played out, and the road took to the gulch side, making room for a placer mine. The mine pit was deep and long, lighted by pitch torches. Chinese were at work carrying baskets of gravel on shoulder poles up ladders and plank scaffoldings to the headbox of a sluice where a watchman sat in a lookout shanty with a shotgun poked from the window.

Far away now were the sounds of the camp. He could hear no pursuit. He rode, jogging easily, his hat back, the horse's movements bumping out the words of his song:

> "Co-man-che John is a highwayman
>   He hails from County Pike,
> And whenever he draws his Navies out
>   'Tis share and share alike."

CHAPTER ELEVEN

THE WAGON TRAIN WAS ENCAMPED on the flats near Crowfoot River. There was a fine campfire, and he could recognize shadows moving near it. Mary Bird was there, and he had promised to return her to her people.

He reined in and sat while freshening his chew of tobacco, but White Eyes had mentioned her and ambush both in the same breath, and he decided to ride on. She would be better off with Prudence Browers. If anyone tried to harm the girl, Prudence Browers would hit him with that horse pistol of hers, and turn him so the hair side was in.

> "Now, John lit out for Kansas
>   With a pal named Injun Ike,
> A very shady char-ac-ter
>   Who'd jumped his bail in Pike;
> They fought John Brown in Pawnee town,
>   And the camp of Liber-tee,
> They fought through the election
>   On the side of slaver-ee."

That night he spread his blankets within sound of the river current. With the first sign of dawn, he headed northward through low mountains. After camping a second night, he observed, as he traveled, that the timber was giving way to sage. Crossing a minor divide, he struck the Missouri, and followed it downstream, keeping clear of Confederate Gulch and Last Chance, both strongholds of the vigilance committee, and again found himself in mountain forest. He replenished his supplies at a tiny placer camp and, still going northward, reached a country where massive snow-deep mountains rose from the plains. He found Indian encampments long abandoned. It was the land of the Blackfeet, who had moved across the Plains in the summer buffalo hunt.

He prospected for gold, working his way up a nameless river, from tributary to tributary, without turning a color. The mountains grew steeper, until he was in a land of hanging valleys, glaciers, and lakes as cold as ice. At a lonely village of Piegans, he traded one of his extra pistols for a packhorse and a bag of Indian meal, then crossed the deep snow of another pass and reached a river flowing toward the Pacific.

Indians became more numerous. He camped at fishing villages, still going north, asking along the way about the fabulous mountain of the bloodstones—the mountain of rubies.

He was inside Canada. He traded another pistol for two ruby-red arrowheads, and courted the widow of a Flathead chieftain who claimed to know the secret; but she departed, taking with her his bowie, his extra shirt, and his stewpot. He kept going. He was robbed of his packhorse by Kutenais, and he lost all else except his scalp, his horse, and his guns to a raiding party of Bloods. Weary and half starved, he joined a fur trader's caravan on Natoose Lake.

The trader was a French breed, named Laroque, who spoke no English. They conversed in the Chinook jargon. Laroque traded for beaver, mink, and marten skins on a sliding scale—a half-pint of whisky for the first pelt, regardless of its quality, with the price becoming progressively less as drunkenness overcame his customers.

With the packhorses laden and the last demijohn of whisky gone, they turned south, crossed the boundary, rode through the hill country of the Palouse, and once again Comanche John looked on Snake River.

He stopped briefly at Maycamp, Gold Hill, and Injun Diggings, all placer camps beyond their peak. He dickered with an itinerant jeweler over the two arrowheads, only to learn that they had been chipped from scarlet bottle glass.

Sadly he rode the Orofino freight road. He stopped at a sheebang for a friendly drink with the proprietor, but the whisky tasted of Indian nightshade.

With pistol drawn, he said: "I'm a religious man, having given up the ways of sin, including robbery, but I say that them as tries to feed a man the Injun drug and rob

him during the night is the next lowest thing to an abolitionist. I reckon you got a cache o' gold hid out under the
floor, and when I ride off I'm taking it."

Comanche John entered Orofino more prosperous than
he had been in a twelvemonth. He increased his fortune
in a faro game. Together with a man in a fancy vest, he
formed a partnership to operate a toll road between Cliff
Ferry and Goldenleaf over Emigrant Pass, but his partner
departed one night with their entire capital.

"I'll git my stake yet," John vowed to a prospector,
named Snakebite Owen, who took him in and fed him. "I
mean a *real* stake. Hundred thousand, two hundred thousand. Maybe a million. Yep, that's the ticket, a million
dollars! Gypsy gal told me. They practice witchcraft,
gypsies; and when they look into your future they do it
through the whole deck, right down to the case cyards.
She said I was fated to die a country squire, rich and ree-
spected, in bed, with my boots off, and my Navies hung
up on the bedpost. Ye see, I *know* I'm a-going to git it;
the only question is *when*. Now, it might be soon, or it
might be late."

Snakebite Owen was frying sourdough flapjacks on a
piece of smoking sheet metal. He said: "I know about a
vein where we'd make a million, maybe *two* million, only
it's in quartzite, and it jumps around some, following the
bedding planes. It'll take capital to open it up."

"Then we'll *git* the capital to open it up."

He crossed a mountain pass that even then, in late summer, held traces of snow. He gave no more thought to
Owen's million. All prospectors have a million-dollar vein
somewhere. He dropped down on Clearwater through
magnificent cliffs and tall straight forest. He reached
Poverty Bar, scene of a month-old gold rush. It was a
camp of shanties and wickiups where all commodities
came in by muleback, with flour selling at $1.50 a pound.

He walked the crooked, narrow street, and heard a familiar sound—the banjo and hoarse voice of White Eyes blended in song:

"I got a gal in Natchez
And a wife with yaller hair
But I'd trade 'em both
For a brown-eyed lass
From the lodge of the Del-a-ware."

John came close to the log and canvas saloon where the blind man had posted himself. He muttered, "Delaware? I'll take a Blackfeet for mine."

White Eyes almost dropped his banjo. Then he commenced stamping his boots and whanging the banjo in strident rhythm, but John stopped him.

"Here, now. None o' that doggerel about me. My life has been peaceful of late. Nobody around here gives a thought to Comanche John, and I don't care to remind 'em. How are things back in Montana?"

"They took out an eighty-pound nugget at Diamond, and one whole side of the street burned at Last Chance, but it was built again a week later. Say, what was it you gave young Billy McCormick?"

"It war nothing. Just a wuthless piece of dumpite, why?"

"Wuthless!" White Eyes cackled.

"I *reckoned* it war wuthless. Why, what'd ye hear?"

"Wuthless rock that'll lead 'em to a million dollars. *Two* million, maybe."

"Now, White Eyes. You been listening to crazy prospector talk. I just left a prospector yonder on the Snake River side that figured he had a million three feet ahead of his drill point, but—"

"Why else would Gar Robel go in partnership with him?"

His eyes narrowed. "What are you talking about?"

"Why, what I been trying to tell you. They went in together, Gar Robel and young Billy McCormick, and from what I hear it all started over some piece of rock you delivered to him. To Billy. Gar found out about it. Him, and that big Pike's Peaker with the wagon train—"

"Buffalo Browers?"

"Yes, Browers. They're all in together."

"Wuthless dumpite," John said, but he no longer showed any conviction. He chewed, and thought back. "Come all the way from I-dee-ho after it," he muttered. "Kilt Dakotah for it. Tried to kill me for it." And he asked, "Whar be they now?"

"I hear they camped at Yallerstone Landing."

"No gold in *that* country."

White Eyes cackled, "No gold. Listen to him! Only a million in gold, sunk somewhere beneath the river."

"Paddy McCormick's?"

"Of course, Paddy McCormick's. The same gold he tried to haul away downriver when he got distrustful of the express company; the gold he got kilt for; the gold that was sunk and never found."

"Couple a thousand ounces, maybe. But a million—"

"I say closer to *two* million. Three-quarters of the gold that Paddy sluiced off Irishman's Bar; and next to Eldorado, the Irishman's was the richest in Bonanza."

"Tell me about that river robbery—what they know."

"Why, he sneaked off, Paddy did, secret. Tried to move his gold downriver himself in a mackinaw boat without the road agents knowing of it. Figured he'd float it down the Yallerstone. But they found out and attacked. He put up a fearsome fight, I hear, and in the end the powder blowed. Anyhow, there war an explosion heered all the way to the Sage Creek trading post. They seen the fire from there, but night had settled, and in the morning there wasn't a sign of anything. Never has been a sign of anything. Picked Paddy up on shore. He'd swum that far, and give out. Bullet *here*." He tapped his breast. "Hauled him to Yallerstone Landing. Out of his head. Lot o' wild talk. Died two weeks later."

"Didn't they find the wreck?"

"Not an inch of her. You know why?" White Eyes leaned forward and got hold of John's buckskin vest. "I'll tell ye. The *gold* pulled her down. The weight of the gold. And the weight of the gold is *holding* her thar. Two million in gold! Five ton!"

"And now Gar figures to deal himself in on all of it!" John hitched his Navies. "Ye know, all of a sudden I'm struck with the itch to visit Montana."

White Eyes did a jig and giggled. "Same old Comanche. Right back to spit in the cougar's eye."

"I'll be in no danger. I warn't born to be hung. Gypsy gal in Denver City told me so."

White Eyes chorded the banjo and sang:

> "Co-man-che rode to Denver town
> As bold as bold could be,
> He laid his hard-won money down
> For rum and raw whis-kee."

"Never mind that pesky song. Sometimes I think that song's the main cause of my trouble. Every damn' sheriff trying to write the last verse to it, and git famous."

"If *Gar* ever gives ye trouble, just ask him about the Eagletop Massacre."

"We all suspected, but it can't be proved."

"It can now! They caught up with Lightnin' Bob Galt, and hung him. In Lewiston. Judge and twelve-man jury. Say, it *war* a fancy trial. Confessed all. Broke down and turned yellow as a Yankee being chased by Beauregard. That's what I hear. I hear he confessed who the rest of the gang was, too."

"Robel? Black Dave? Sellers?" John asked eagerly.

"I can't say, but I'll wager Robel won't be back around the Snake River diggings for a while. If he does, he'll stay permanent."

"Waal, now!" John chewed it over. "Why, White Eyes, that seems to put Gar and me on a new footing. I go back thar now, I'll wager he'd forget all about me being Comanche John. So he's made a partnership with young Billy McCormick to find two million in gold. White Eyes, reach your hand out here and have yourself a feel of their third partner!"

CHAPTER TWELVE

IT WAS LATE AFTERNOON, and very hot on the eastern slope of the Montana mountains. For many miles John had followed the ruts of a freight road down a dry coulee bottom. Slowly, as it approached the Yellowstone, the coulee widened. Until recently the bottoms had been heavily overgrown by large cottonwoods, but now only stumps and brush remained; the timber had been taken to build rafts and mackinaw boats for downstream journeys to Fort Union and Saint Louis.

At last he had his first view of the river and the town.

The Yellowstone was low, with grayish mudbars showing through. The town was a huddle of log buildings on a bench overlooking a single dock and a warehouse. A freight wagon, with its team unhitched, stood by the loading platform. There was no movement anywhere.

It was a strange sight after the boom-camp activity that Comanche John had just left behind, and he stopped to rest his right leg around the saddle horn, regarding it from beneath the dust-coated brim of his black slouch hat.

He sat for a long ten minutes. A breeze reached him, carrying the damp of the river and the stink of buffalo hides being tanned at some Indian lodges on the downstream bend. Beyond the lodges he could see still another camp, some white-topped wagons, and a shanty or two, distorted by heat waves that rose from the baked sage flats.

He spoke to his pony and rode on. The main street was a continuation of the freight road. It was dry-rutted and hard as cement from the wheels of wagons that had traveled it during the wet weather of June. He glanced in a watering trough, and found it dry.

One saloon and a general store were still open, and a couple of men had come as far as the awning of the store to look at him.

"Howdy," John said. "This seems to be a quiet day in the camp o' Yellowstone Landing."

The proprietor, a lean, close-mouthed man said, "It's tolerable."

John spat a stream of tobacco juice in the road.

The contempt visible in the action led the man to say: "We do our share of business here at the Landing, never you fear. Yellowstone takes a back seat to nobody. Give us three more years and get the quartz mines at Bonanza to producing, and we'll handle more river freight than Benton. Only, right now the river's down. You should have seen us in June. Street so jammed with freight outfits you couldn't have found *room* to spit."

"Steamboats come this far?"

"They make it to Ratling Creek. Unload to keelboats there. Hell of a lot easier than that wagon trip from Benton to Last Chance, if you want my estimate."

John gave the appearance of listening, but his eyes kept moving toward the camp downriver.

"What's yonder?"

"That's the McCormick party."

"Prospectors?"

"Say, you must be a stranger from way off if you can't guess what *they're* looking for."

The other man then spoke up, "Irishman's gold. Fifth bunch this year come looking for the treasure."

And they both laughed, indicating that the search had become a joke in Yellowstone, and that probably there *was* no treasure.

"Why," said John, squinting against the heat wave, "they seem to be working on a mackinaw boat. What's their names?"

"I don't know their names except for Robel and McCormick. They wanted credit, but damned if *I'd* extend 'em credit."

The second said: "One of 'em they call Black Dave. He's the one got drunk and shot out Lige's new window."

Comanche John reared up in the saddle. "Black Dave is dead!"

"Not *this* Black Dave, though I do admit it would be a good deed to end the summer with."

In his mind's eye John could see Black Dave hit by Navy lead and knocked over the rump of his horse; but some men die hard, like tomcats.

He said, "Thank-ee," and rode on, muttering to himself: "It ain't like me to git a man broadside and have him pick himself up again. My eye ain't what it used to be, that's a fact. And I been getting a stiffness in my wrist. I say it's coming my time o' life to get a stake together and settle down."

He watered his pony at the river, then rode downstream, skirting the brush. The sun was getting low. He was beyond the stink of the Indian camp, and a breeze carried to his nostrils the odor of cooking onions and freshly baked bread. After a day of riding, it made him feel weak in the middle.

"That's stew. And not only that, it's old-fashioned *Missouri* stew. By grab, thar's only one person in this territory cooks stew with a smell like that, and that's Mrs. Browers. She *is* here, sure enough."

He touched his bootheels to the pony's side, and galloped the last quarter-mile. Five wagons stood in a circle, with a shanty and a brush lean-to beyond. A woman, tall and erect, stood shading her eyes against the sunset, watching him. The woman was Prudence Browers.

He urged the horse faster. Departed now was his slouched posture. He rode as gallantly as a young colonel leading the charge. Wheeling with a tight rein that made the gunpowder rear and paw with his front feet, he swept off his old slouch hat.

"Mrs. Browers," he cried. "When I smelt that stew, I knew who it be, because nobody this side o' Pike County, Missouri, could concoct anything like it."

She was tight-mouthed and hard-eyed. "Comanche John!"

"Now, hold your temper—"

"Yes, ye be Comanche John. I knew it the first night back at the wagon train, and I know it now."

The grandeur went out of John's posture. He sat with his head bowed, his hat clasped over his breast, the evening breeze stirring some locks of his unroached hair.

"Ma'am, it's true. I been a black sheep that strayed from the fold. I been a gunman and a road agent, and I been wicked to shame Gomorrah. But, thanks be to glory, I met up with a preacher that showed me the arrers of my ways, and I hit the sawdust trail to glory. I did, for a fact, and I've engaged in no robbery to amount to much in these two long and poverty-riddled years."

She relented enough to say, "You're hungry, I suppose."

"I'm hungry as a stray wolf in Janawary."

She grumbled and looked around: "Well, I dunno. I'm only the cook and scullion around here. I'm afeard when that Robel sees ye thar'll be bloodshed."

"Don't worry about me. I'll take care—"

"I ain't worried about you!" she shouted. "It's Robel that's *paying* us."

Her husband was coming. "Maw, who's there?"

"Old friend o' yours," she answered wearily.

"You!" Buffalo saw him, and came to a halt. "You got nothing to come here for."

John thought it over. He looked around and saw Mary Bird peeping from the rear opening of a wagon.

"Nothing to come for, he says. Now that's a matter of opinion. It might be that I came about the Injun gal."

"She's safe enough without you."

"With *Robel* around?"

"He's been a gentleman. Every minute he has. And as for him *buying* her, well he explained how that was—"

"Ask *her* how it was."

The girl knew that she had been seen. She leaned from the wagon. She was prettier than he had remembered.

She cried to John: "No, you go 'way. Mary Bird don't go back. Mary Bird don' want go to Canada."

Buffalo said triumphantly: "You hear that? She don't want you around, so git a-going."

John chewed and spat, showing his ill temper. He pulled his old slouch hat back down over his eyes. He touched a heel to the ribs of the pony and rode at an amble, around the wagons, toward a lean-to that had been built against a low cutbank. Men were outside, watching him. He knew one of them: Gar Robel.

John kept the sun at his back. A man was a poor target with the sun behind him. He kept himself in the sun by pointing his shadow. He kept riding, taking it as easy as he could. A couple of men were crouched in the shady depths of the lean-to at Robel's back.

Robel, sun-blinded, moved and held a hand out to shade his eyes, still not sure who John was. Then he drew up and stood, big and high-shouldered, with his studhorse legs wide-set, and his hands driven down on his hips above the butts of his smooth-bore buckshot pistols.

Fred Sellers and the hawk-faced man came up. Billy Mc-Cormick and someone John did not recognize were hurrying toward them. Now he could see who was in the lean-to. One was filthy Tom Claus, and the other, sure enough, was Black Dave. So he had lived, John's bullet notwithstanding. He also recognized Kabo, Wolf Jake, and Morrison. Dave had his sawed-off shotgun as usual, so John pulled up out of its range.

"Howdy, lads," he said. "How's your health? All sewed up and healed?" He chuckled and spat, then wiped his lips on the back of his hand and thoughtfully contemplated them. "Now, I *am* glad, because I wanted ye in good shape for our partnership."

"*What?*" cried Robel.

"Our partnership. I was meaning to tell ye. We're partners in this, hunting the river for Paddy McCormick's gold."

Incredulity made Gar Robel stare at him for a moment. Then he recovered himself enough to laugh. He laughed loudly, derisively.

John sat through it patiently. Then he said: "Been in I-dee-ho. I hear news about an old friend of yours. Business associate. Lightnin' Bob Galt. They caught up with him. Gave him a trial. Twelve men and judge. Oh, they be doing things up fancy in I-dee-ho these days. Only, the result was the same—ten feet o' stiff rope, and nothing to stand on."

"They hung Bob Galt?"

"Yep."

"Why tell *me* about it?"

"I was getting to that. He war repentant. Told all about the Eagletop Massacre. Who all was in with him. He warn't the leader, o' course, but he told who the leader was. You heered of him, Gar, only I'm not mentioning any names."

The derision was gone from Robel's face. He waited for John to go on, his jaw set, muscles knotted, fists clenched, and shoulders sloped forward. Comanche sat his horse easily.

"Told it all, how him and the others ambushed that pack train and kilt 'em. Oh, that country yonder is riled up. And that young U.S. Marshal—they got a new one, ye know. He swears he'd go any place for the rest of that gang, if he found out whar they be. I guess he'd come to Montana, even. It came to my mind that I *knew* whar they were—some of 'em. But then I rode off, forgetting to let him know. Afterward I'd have writ him a letter, only my eddication was never such as included the three R's. But when I got to Alder—say, I'm not making ye weary with all this? You ain't listening just to be polite?"

"What did you do in Alder?"

"Oh, that. Why, I hired a letter writ. Told that U.S. Marshal whar they all were, what they was up to. Put a postal on it. But it didn't git mailed. I left it behind, with a friend of mine, telling him to send it along in case I got kilt on this trip, or in case I just didn't show up."

Robel relaxed enough to take a deep, deep breath.

John, scratching at his neck where the whiskers were scraggly, said: "Can't make trouble for my partners, ye know. That ain't my style. Make trouble for them as makes trouble for me. Share and share alike, that's my motto."

CHAPTER THIRTEEN

COMANCHE JOHN, WITH HIS STOMACH FILLED, sat behind the cookwagon. He played casino with Billy McCormick, lost $7, and agreed with Prudence Browers on the evils of gambling.

"Repent ye," he said, "for the Day of Judgment is at hand. 'Will ye be caught on the riffles of righteousness, or will ye be washed down the tailings to hell!' Thar was a *sermon*. Parson delivered it. The Reverend Jeremiah Parker, the same sky pilot that plucked me out o' the black gulch o' sin and made me the upstanding Christian gent'man ye see before ye tonight. By grab, Prudence, if you and me and that Parson ever throwed in together we could reform the Territory, with maybe a chunk o' I-dee-ho tossed in."

The fire died. Tired men were already going to bed. He could hear the river, now, a quiet sound, deep and full.

Billy McCormick stood up, stretched his big youthful body, laughed for no reason, and said he was going to hit the shucks. John then asked about the bit of whitish rock he had given him in Bonanza, and Billy, still yawning, said, ho hum, that he placed more faith in Mr. Garrick and his instrument of science, which was said to be magnetic to gold.

John had observed the arrival of Garrick earlier in the evening. He was a thin, grayish man of fifty, with a sharp face and protruding eyeballs. The "instrument" was inside a black leather portmanteau which Garrick kept continually beside him, and under lock and key.

"I've seen 'em," John said. "In Californy. Call 'em doodlebugs. A professor somebody had one; he was using it on those high and dry gravels by Redbone City. But it war too delicate, and kept pinting out ground that only gave up with half a cent to the pan. Who's got that bit of white rock now?"

"Robel."

"Ye should never have given it to him, lad."

"We're all in this together."

"Ay."

John got up, hitched the heavy belts with their Navies, and sauntered along the riverbank. The mackinaw boat was there, rocking gently in the current, and he stopped to look at it. It floated, but it was little better than a raft. In its center was an opening onto the river, and over it a tripod of timbers with a block designed to take heavy rope. A pump was bolted beside it, and on shore were three hogsheads and a segment of steam boiler such as he had seen used in California to explore bedrock when it lay beneath water level.

He turned, his right hand by habit on the Navy, when he heard a bootstep on the shore behind him. It was Robel.

"We'll have to agree on a few things, John."

"Such as?"

"Our split of the gold—if we find it."

"How'd it stand before I came?"

"Three ways—Billy, myself, and Garrick. That is, if Garrick's instrument detects it."

John laughed, spat, and said, "If."

"If not, he won't get a color."

"Whar does Browers and those wagoners come in?"

"Straight wages. I'll give them enough for a grubstake in the farming business."

"You'll give it? Out of your own pocket?"

Robel nodded.

"That's generous. I guess I can afford to be generous, too. But not *too* generous." John stopped chewing. His jaw had taken a hard set, and his eyes were narrowed to slits. "Gar, I'll tell ye how it is with me. I traveled a steep, far piece since the year o' Forty-nine, sleeping on the ground, dodging bullets and hangman's ropes; but now I'm getting old for the business, and I aim to settle down. But I ain't going Injun, and I ain't going back to Pike County and sleep with the hawgs in the bottoms. No, I aim to ree-tire in style, in store clothes, in a house with windows and a floor in it. I aim to *make my stake*. I aim to git it *here*. Some folks say thar's a million dollars sunk in the river. Some say two million. Either way, it'll split up into great big chunks by a several. When I leave, it'll be with a packhorse—and I'll have all the gold I can carry on its back. Share and share alike, that's my motto."

Robel, watching him closely through the darkness, said, "You already know where it is."

"The treasure? You ain't accusing *me* of that bit o' piracy. I waren't in on it. I war on Fraser River at the time, or at Yallerjack."

"You know where it is, but you can't get it by yourself. You need men and equipment."

"Gar, I've seen Nevady jackasses that talked more sense than you."

"What did Dakotah tell you before he died?"

"Nary a thing."

"What was in that parfleche?"

"Clothes and truck. And that white bit of rock."

Gar took a step forward. His temper, long held down, was threatening to get away from him. His jaw muscles worked.

"I'm not a fool. I know there was something that you kept for yourself. Now maybe you think you can win those wagoners and that dumb Irishman over on your side, and beat me out of the swag, me and my boys. But you won't. Now tell me what you found out from Dakotah!"

John scratched his whiskers. He itched between the shoulders, too. He backed against the hogsheads and rubbed with the added satisfaction that he was protected from any guns behind him.

"Why, that war months ago. Months and months. It'll take some recollecting, but I'll likely remember, on our way upriver."

Comanche John that night slept soundly. Gar would not shoot him. Not *that* night or the next. Gar would not let him carry to his grave the secret which he thought Dakotah had imparted.

"Understand Gar Robel's paying ye out of his own pocket," he said to Prudence the next morning. "Or is it promise now and collect next fall?"

"We'll collect, never fear."

"It surprises me no little that ye'd do business with a whisky drinker and hangman like that."

"Go on, eat your victuals. Lick your plate, and quit trying to stir trouble in this camp."

He chuckled and said: "Ye know, Prudence, I like your style. I been thinkin' of building me a cabin and settling down. If it waren't for that pesky husband of yours, danged if I wouldn't make a bride out of ye."

She seized a broom which she'd been using to sweep the hard-baked gumbo around the cookwagon, and came in long strides, with her dress billowing.

"Git to moving!" she bellowed. "Shake your hocks, you shif'less, dirty, tobacco-chewing outlaw. Cockleburrs in your hair you ain't combed since Oregon!" He'd cleared out a safe distance, and she waved the broom after him.

"Think I'd trade you for a fine, upstanding man like Mr. Browers?"

John had lost his hat, and now he sneaked back after it. "Ornery woman!" he grumbled. "Ruther have a Blackfoot. Never see a Blackfoot sweep a man right out o' the teepee."

He noticed Mary Bird nearby, looking at him. The others who had seen the incident were still laughing among themselves, but the Indian girl merely watched him with eyes that were dark and serious.

He said: "Yes, I would. I'd pick me a Blackfeet. I'd pick me a gal like you, if I was ten, twelve year younger. By dang, maybe I'm not too old anyhow. Plenty men my age find themselves a young squaw."

"No good," said Mary Bird.

"Ye mean white men? Ye mean ye'd rather marry an Injun?"

"White man all right. *Young* white man heap good."

"Oh, so that's it. McCormick. So that's why ye wanted to come along and not go north to your people."

"You talk to young white man for Mary Bird, hey?"

"Me do it? Tell him he ought to marry ye? I'll be danged if I will. I want ye for myself."

He sat alone, on a sidehill, and watched the camp. Prudence was hanging dishtowels up to dry on a line strung between a wagon and a box-elder tree. Browers, a skilled man with tools, headed a crew of six who were putting the mackinaw boat in final shape for the journey downriver. At Robel's camp a game of three-card monte was in progress until the sun grew hot, then two of the men left with packhorses in search of game, and the others went lazily to work getting supplies aboard. During the afternoon Spotsy Huss drove down in a light rig with a hundred-pound coil of rope for which he had made the long, rough journey to Bonanza. He saw John, and his surprise made him almost fall from the wagon. Then he sat down, rigidly grasping the sides of the seat, and cried in a magpie voice:

"Keep your hands away from those guns. Shoot me and you'll swing for it."

John said, "Spotsy, I've gone out for bigger game than you with a handful of rocks."

Big Buffalo Browers moved between them, saying: "It's all right, Spotsy. We're just laboring for pay. Robel says he comes, so he comes."

At grubpile that night Comanche John sat watching Mary Bird as she moved in her lithe, silent manner around the cookfire. She was a capable girl, quick to learn a white woman's ways, and it was good to watch her do things without false movements and wasted effort. Something made him glance around, and there was Gar Robel in the shadow between two of the wagons, staring at her.

Robel did not realize he had been noticed, although John's eyes remained on him for four or five minutes, so rapt he was in every move the girl made.

It had been a good supper, but the heel of it had grown grease-hardened in his plate, and suddenly John did not want any more. He tossed it out, wiped the plate with grass, and ambled over to where Billy McCormick was seated.

"Fine gal," he said, hunkering on the heels of his jack boots, "Mary Bird."

Billy laughed, as he laughed about everything, and said, "She is that."

"One thing about an Injun gal, Billy, she knows her place. None o' this beating a man over the head with a broom. By grab, that ornery Browers woman wouldn't last ten day in a Blackfeet camp. No, she wouldn't. They'd shave her hair off and throw her in the river."

He walked between the wagons toward Robel, and

Robel, seeing him approach, pretended to be otherwise occupied.

John stopped and said, "We had this out a long time ago, up at Sheebang City, remember?"

It angered Robel to learn that his interest in the Indian girl had been observed. His voice was low but intense.

"You rode away with her. You had her to yourself for a week. Now maybe you think you *own* her."

"I don't cotton to that ree-mark. Mary Bird is good and true, and I treated her as such."

Robel laughed with a hard jerk of his shoulders. "She's an Injun."

"Some Injuns are might' near as good as humans, I reckon. *Better'n* some humans. As long as I'm here, and as long as Prudence is here—"

"I've stayed away from her, haven't I?"

John looked at him with narrow speculation. "So that's it! *That's* why ye went out of your way to hire Browers and those wagoners o' his. That's why ye paid 'em from your own purse—because that way they'd come and bring the gal."

"I get what I start after. You ought to know that from California."

"The point is, which do ye want the worst—two million in gold or that gal?"

"Which do I want *first*. I'll take the gold first." He turned away, nudging John with his elbow. "And after that—well, I'll play you a hand of monte for her."

John watched him go, and muttered: "Not with me. You'll play that hand with the devil. I reckon you played your hand with the devil, and the devil won already."

CHAPTER FOURTEEN

JOHN RODE THE RIVER. He spent one night at a trapper's shanty, the next at the fur-trading post on Sage Creek. In the morning he stood on a hill overlooking the Yellowstone, while the half-breed trader, supplementing his poor English with the Indian sign language, told of that night, more than a year before, when he had heard the shooting, the deep roar of the explosion, and had sighted through the midnight darkness a distant, drifting fire.

"And ye looked in the morning?" John asked.

"At dawn. Look long tam. All day. No boat. Only two dead men washed in rivaire brush. Shot. I bury them." Then he asked, laughing, "You look for gold, too?"

"And you're telling me thar ain't any?"

"Who knows? Perhaps, perhaps not."

John rode on, following first one bank and then the other, imagining the attack, the battle, the drifting, fire-gutted wreck. The gold would eventually have sunk her. It would hold the hulk fast to the bottom, year after year, until the timbers rotted and were washed off by the floods of spring, leaving the gold behind. And there it would stay, sinking deeper and deeper in the mud, and no one would ever find it, unless the stream changed her course and some farmer like Buffalo Browers drove his plow through it as he'd seen old pieces of keelboat plowed up when he was a boy, in Missouri. But even that wasn't likely, because by that time the mines would be worked out and the country would be turned back to the Indians.

He rode much farther than he had intended, and

reached the ferry where wagon outfits had been crossing, taking the short-cut road from the Big Horn to Fort Benton. The express rider passed while he was there, and John returned upriver, saddened by the war news, for it was the dark days of Petersburg. He knew that someone had been following him, but he did not bother his mind about it. He knew well enough that Robel would have him watched.

He got back to camp in time for the final turmoil, when the mackinaw boat set out downriver, and the wagons, loaded with supplies, struck out across the rough river bluffs toward the Sage. It was a difficult, roadless journey, and impossible beyond the Sage, where the wagons were left behind, and the supplies hauled piecemeal by packhorse to Brule Bottoms, where Gar Robel had decided to headquarter the search.

They built shanties of jack pine, which grew spottily on the hills, and men on the mackinaw boat commenced probing the river bottom, hunting the sunken wreck. It was still hot in the afternoon sun, but the days had grown shorter, and with night came a frosty reminder of winter. There were other signs of the season's lateness: the river had risen slightly, while in the distance the mountains had new snow, the alders were yellow, and the gulches were filled with purple haze.

Each morning Garrick left camp carrying his portmanteau, and floated off downstream in one of the clumsy, flat-bottomed skiffs to test the river; but after his first few journeys the camp lost faith in him, and his "doodlebug" became an object of ridicule. The real search was being done from the mackinaw boat.

From her deck, as she lay anchored in midriver, men probed with hooks and pike poles. When something was found of a hopeful size and shape, it was raised by means of heavy tackle and the grapple. In instances when the grapple failed, it was explored through the hogshead caisson, which could be lowered through the center well, weighted down, and its water pumped out.

One evening eleven men arrived from down the river. They were tough, tired, and purposeful. They ate, and said little, and had a long look around while John, hunkered in the brush shadow, read vigilante sign all over them. But they were not looking for him, nor for Robel, who spent a few uneasy hours also. They had hanged two members of a sluice-robber gang at the mouth of Redwillow, and were on the trail of four more. After a while they left, riding into the twilight toward Sage Creek trading post, and John followed them until they headed northward for Sixmile diggings, or Confederate Gulch.

He slept in the pocket end of a cutbank, with a fire for warmth, and arose stiff from cold at the first gray of morning. He rode to the river. A faint mist hung over it, and the brush along both shores was shadowy-black. He glimpsed movement. A man was pushing a skiff into the water. It was Justinn Garrick, and John wondered how Garrick had got so far from Brule at that hour. Later, John found where he had slept beneath a brush lean-to.

"Doodlebugging," he said.

Back at camp, with no one around, he entered the shanty where Garrick's belongings were stored. There, inside an old carpetbag, he found the "doodlebug," an intricate, incomprehensible mass of magnets, pendulums, and coiled wire. He put it back as he had found it, then waited until Garrick returned at night, tired and muddy, and carrying his portmanteau.

"I'd give a plenty to look at that gold detector ye got thar," John said. "Why is it ye keep it hid?"

Garrick answered coldly, "One must sign a pledge of secrecy before he is allowed to use the Dr. Glendennin

Gold and Precious Metals Detector."

John lay in his bed and pretended to sleep. After the camp had long been quiet, he got up and strapped on his Navies. Barefoot, trying to avoid cactus, he took the long way round through brush shadow to the shanty. He stood at the door and listened. He could hear the heavy breathing of men. He had no way of knowing if Garrick were asleep. He had to gamble on it. He stepped inside.

It was dark. After the night freshness, it seemed hot and fetid. He took a step, groping. His toe touched a bedroll made out on the floor. He found the wall, and took another step. The portmanteau was there, and Garrick was asleep beside it. John lifted it. It was lighter than he expected. Something inside gave a muffled, metallic rattle. The man beside him turned, and the regularity of his breathing was interrupted. John stood still, waiting, and the breathing became regular again. Then, carrying the portmanteau, he backed outside. He filled his lungs, and blew. Sweat ran down his forehead, and he wiped it away. There was still no alarm. All were asleep. He unfastened the lock of the portmanteau, using the tip of his bowie.

Inside were some small tools, a grapple, some rope, a pistol, some odds and ends of clothing, a copy of *The Tragedy of King Lear,* and in the bottom a can so heavily weighted it gave the impression of being fastened to the bottom. With a grunt and a delighted chuckle he lifted it out and unfastened the top. The dim moonlight played dully yellow over gold.

He took out a four-finger pinch of coarse gold the size of oatmeal, nuggets like flattened pebbles. He let them fall to his other hand, and they made a slightly metallic rattle. He rolled them back and forth, liking the cold weight of the gold. A noise startled him. He stood, not breathing. He had dropped the pinch of gold in his pocket, and his hands were on his Navies.

It was only young Harum, Billy's boy, that night riding sentry, stopping to pour a cup of tea from the bucket that was kept hot by the stone fireplace.

He waited through long minutes until the youth had finished and ridden away. Then he hurriedly repacked the portmanteau, carried it back inside, and placed it in its old position against the wall. He was once again in his blankets before it came to him that he had left the lock unfastened. He cursed himself, but he did not return.

He slept, a hair-trigger sleep, and awoke with the realization that someone was walking down the path to the water. The moon was gone, but there was a faint grayness of dawn from the horizon and the river. A man was silhouetted, pushing a skiff into the current. It was Garrick. In another five minutes John was mounted, and following along the shore.

CHAPTER FIFTEEN

THE BOAT TRAVELED TOO SWIFTLY for him, and he lost sight of it. He forded the river and took the short route, across a bend to the spot where Garrick's camp was located. He was not there. He had gone straight on, and it was only by chance that John glimpsed him in the yellow glare of sunrise far downstream.

He rode and watched. The day grew hot. There were riders across the river. Thinking of vigilantes, he hid his horse in a draw and watched, belly down, from a clump of junipers; but the riders proved to be Robel's men: Claus, Sellers, Black Dave, and the hawk-faced one, Wally Claven.

The sun made him sleepy. He napped until the afternoon cooled, then he ambled back to Garrick's hidden camp.

Garrick returned at dusk, rowing hard against the current, and hid his skiff in the brush. He was seated cross-legged, munching biscuit and jerky, when John came up afoot and spoke to him. The man jumped, twisting on all fours, grabbing for a little pocket pistol, but John, with a shoulder hitch and flip of his expert wrist had already unholstered a Navy.

"No, I ain't looking to burn powder. Put your gun down."

Garrick stiffly obeyed. Then he got control of himself, drew erect, his thin face contemptuous, a smile bending the outer corners of his mouth.

"Practicing your profession!"

"Why, yes, this *is* my profession." He hefted the Navy, looked at it, and dropped it back in the leather. "Every man to his own talents, I say. Share and share alike, that's my motto." He scratched his whiskers, and looked at the portmanteau. "Now, for instance, if we was hungry, and if I had a haunch of venison, which I ain't, I'd whack it in half with ye." He moved over and nudged the portmanteau with the toe of his jack boot. "Show me the doodlebug."

Garrick laughed. It was a surprised laugh. "You mean you came down here with a gun in your hand for *that?*"

"That, and other things, so show it to me."

"Don't be a fool, man, there is no doodlebug."

"Not in the portmanteau, I'll grant. But I'll tell ye what thar *is* in it—and that's gold. Yep, a can o' yaller gold. Nuggets, and coarse stuff, the same as come off Irishman's Bar in Bonanza, eight hundred fine, which is passing good, but not up to Bannack. The same gold that Paddy McCormick lost beneath the waters."

"You're insane!"

"Come to think, I got some of that same gold hyar in my pocket. Bad habit I got in Californy, dropping other men's gold in my pocket." He drew out the heavy pinch of coarse dust and nuggets and let it rattle into his palm. "Recognize it? You would if you was a miner. Miner always knows his own gold, his own gulch, anyhow, because the gold from every gulch looks just a mite different. Now, I'll ask ye to empty that portmanteau."

"This has gone far enough."

"Empty it out!"

John's voice, the sudden narrowing of his eyes, and the slope of his shoulders made the actor jump to obey. He unsnapped the portmanteau's lid, and turned it over, spilling its contents among the autumn litter on the ground. Everything that John had seen the night before was there—except for the can of gold.

He had a look inside, and cried, "Whar is it?"

"I told you—"

"It *war* there last night. A can o' gold. I hefted it. I saw it whilst ye slept. Didn't ye notice the lock warn't fastened?"

"Oh. So *you* were in it."

"Yep, I war."

Garrick spoke through his teeth, "The others, Robel, Claus, how about them?"

"It ain't my policy to bruit things around."

"You told nobody?"

"Not a soul."

Garrick was obviously relieved. He even whistled a popular ditty, "Sweet Baltimore," as he brought order back to his portmanteau.

John said: "So the doodlebug really worked! It really led ye to it."

"The gold detector?" Garrick snapped his fingers. "It was useless. A toy, a gadget. A compass, a very sensitive compass, nothing else. No, I discovered the sunken treasure through use of my powers of observation."

"Ye did?"

"Yes." He cast a derisive gesture up the river. "While *they* toiled and broke their backs like dull-witted brutes, *I* found the spot through the application of reason and intelligence."

"Was it the rock? That whitish rock of Billy's?"

"Let me quote from Marlowe, Christopher Marlowe, who would have been greater than Shakespeare had he not been cut down by the black reaper at the age of twenty-nine. 'A tree,' he said. 'A tree of gold by the waters of Babylon.' Tell me, my good fellow, have you read of Marlowe?"

"I read as much of Marlowe as I have of any man in the whole earth. What do ye mean, 'A tree by the waters of Babylon'?"

But Garrick did not hear him. Standing, his hands spread and his head back in a posture of soliloquy, he quoted Marlowe. Words, rich and incomprehensible, flowed from him:

" '. . . And such conceits as clownage keeps in pay
We'll lead you to the stately tent of war,
Where you shall hear the Scythian Tamburlaine—' "

"The war be going bad, and I want to hear nothing of it. How about that gold? Now ye found it, how do ye expect to raise it without help?"

"Wait! Silence, you will hear me out. I will quote, and you will be my audience. Varlet, I say, draw thy pistol and threaten as you may, but if you kill me then will my secret go to the grave with my body. So listen, then, while I, Justinn Garrick, tragedian and bearer of a famous name, wring tears from your groundling eyes with these few selected passages from the tragedy of *Tamburlaine the Great*."

He started at a low pitch, his voice tremulous; then he built to a climax, and climax upon climax, his voice alternately a scream and a whisper. He pranced around the little brush clearing as words in torrents and volleys rolled from his lips, and John was agape at acting such as he had never seen. Justinn ended, not as Tamburlaine, or even with Marlowe, but as Hamlet the Dane, cut down by a poisoned sword, on one knee, one hand upraised to heaven, the other clasping his forehead: " 'The—rest—is—silence.' "

When John was able to speak, he said: "By grab, I can't for the life of me understand how a man like you ever got stuck out here on this low-down river, mucking for gold. You ought to be in Noo York, with Booth."

"*With* Edwin Booth! That clown? That buffoon? Yes, I *am* an actor, unrecognized, alas, and why? A conspiracy, sir. Those wretched producers, playing hand in glove with mediocrity, closed the doors against me, the very portals. Relegated me to the backwoods circuits until I was forced to the final indignity of playing before black-bearded ruffians in a mining camp." He went on, crouching, gimlet-eyed, whispering: "But I *will* go back, and not empty-handed. I *will* go back, and *buy* their finest theater. There *I* will play what *I* want, *as* I want. 'The play's the thing,' and all the world shall then speak of Justinn Garrick!"

"Why," said John, "I'll come to see ye. I will, for a fact, in a coach and four, with my woman, Prudence, right thar in the seat beside me."

They ate jerky and cold biscuit together, and Comanche John tried to learn the location of the treasure, but all he could get from Garrick was more quotations from Marlowe.

"Five ton o' gold yonder," John reminded him. "You'll need help raising it. You'll have to share sometime with somebody."

"But not now. How long would I live, or *any* of us live, after its location was known?"

"Robel?"

"I tell you, he's a scoundrel. He has no intention of sharing. Once his hands were on the gold, he would kill us all."

"Why, yes. I can see you're a prime judge o' character." He rested on his elbows, and aimed tobacco juice. It was too dark to see if he'd hit. He thought of Robel's men riding the river. "Could be they already know. Could be they seen ye go to it."

"No! He suspects nothing."

"Maybe. Still, a lone hand is dangerous, and ye could use some pardners." He slapped his Navies. "The three of us, me and the Colt brothers. You think it over."

Garrick *was* thinking it over, and John, not wanting to press him, said good night, and rode away.

CHAPTER SIXTEEN

HE DID NOT GO DIRECTLY to the main camp, but circled to the east and came back so that anyone watching his entrance would think he had been at Sage trading post. But the camp seemed to be asleep. His entrance went unnoticed except by the gaunt brindle dog that Chadwaller had picked up at Gros Ventre camp; but the dog quieted after a few howls, and followed John, sniffing and wagging.

Usually, at this time of night, a monte game was in

progress at Black Dave's lean-to, but there, too, everything was dark and quiet. The tea was boiling hot on its hook over the fire. He poured himself a cup. He was hungry. While the tea cooled, he investigated the food shanty, and came out with a pound lump of Prudence's hard sugar. Cracking it with the blade of his bowie, he alternately munched on it and sucked tea through it. He was on his second cup when the sentry rode in. It was the gangling, freckled kid of Harum's—the one they called Beans.

"Hello, Beans," John said, in the same voice he used to quiet a spooky horse. "Come and light. Ye like hard sugar? This is N' Orleans brown, and nigh as good as maple. But say nothing to Prudence. She'd worry, fearing it might ruin our teeth. By the way, have ye seen aught of Robel, or Wally Claven, or any of his boys?"

"I paid no attention."

"How about Claus? Ye can *smell* him. Ain't heered him whoop all night, or did he quit making that chokecherry cordial?"

"He wouldn't raise much fuss tonight nohow. Not since Prudence hit him with the shovel."

"She didn't!" John whispered, aghast.

"She did so. She liked to chop his head off at the shoulders. And she chased off Wolf and Morrison, too."

"I'd of been fond to see that!" He giggled, and did a hunkered-down polka step. Then he grew serious, and laid a hand on the youth's arm. "Beans, you listen to me. Here's some free advice for ye, and it's worth every cent of it. When ye marry, git yourself a Blackfeet gal."

"Like Mary Bird?"

"Why, yes. Like Mary. Except her folks is broke, without a horse to their names, and down to eating buffalo hoof in a patchwork teepee. Git yourself one whose daddy's got plenty o' horses, and then ye'll have some social position to fall into iff'n ye decide to go Injun, as ye might.

122

Thar's worse lives. Just hunt, lie around the teepee, with a squaw to carry ye things. Nobody to chop at ye with a shovel if ye lick up a drop too much chokecherry cordial. O' course I'm not dropping a tear for Tom Claus, him so crawling with graybelly lice he has a whole lean-to to himself."

"She whopped him for fair."

"Ye know, it war my lucky day that she already had a man, or else I'd have wed her just on account of that stew."

"She whopped you too."

"Yes, but not with a *shovel*. Just a broom. A woman does them things to a man she's attracted to so he'll take notice of her." He gnawed brown sugar, which had crystallized as hard as ice. He was uneasy. He could have fared with a dipper of that chokecherry cordial that Claus had been making in a hollowed-out log.

"I wish Ev Glass war here. His singing and fiddle playing war pretty ornery, but it did something to soothe me."

"He was scared you'd kill him."

"On account him giving me away to Gar and them vigilantes? No, I wouldn't shoot a fiddle player. It's bad luck, like shooting a cross-eyed man. And he *could* sing that song about me."

"You ain't the real Comanche John—the one they wrote the song about!"

"Who said?"

"Paw."

"You tell that ignorant paw of yours that sometime I'll cut loose with my Navies and *show* him whether I'm the real Comanche John."

He hunted out his blankets. He kept grumbling: "Not the *real* Comanche. That's how it is with a reputation: gits to spreading, building up, and pretty soon it's out o' hand. Man could be Comanche John, Robbie Lee, and Gineral Beauregard all rolled into one, and still couldn't

123

live *my* rep down. Yep, the signs all pint to one thing— it's time old Comanche John settled down."

He tried to sleep, but he had napped too long during the afternoon, and now sleep would not come to him. He kept listening for the *clip-clop* of returning horses. Suddenly he *knew* that something was wrong. There was no apparent reason; the instinctive certainty simply came to him.

He got out of bed, pulled on his jack boots, which were the only clothing he had removed, and started off at a half-trot for the gunpowder. He changed his mind, knowing that there would be skiffs tied to the float, and that one would get him downstream to Garrick's camp faster. He shoved for midstream, and put his weight to the oars. The camp was quickly behind him.

Things had a different appearance from the stream. Hills, looking like chalk in the moonlight, slid past. He almost overshot Garrick's camp spot, a dark area of brush against a cutbank. He swung sharply against the current, and drove the skiff to shore. He sprang overboard, waded over his ankles, the water flooding with a cold shock through his leaky jack boots, and dragged the skiff, with a grating sound, out of sight through mud and gravel. He stood, getting his breath. In half a minute things became audible. He could hear the river, the slight passage of wind through the brush, the far-away wail of a coyote.

He moved along, hunting a trail, trying to prevent the snap of twigs underfoot. He missed the lean-to, and turned back. He came up against the vertical posts of its rear wall. He stopped again to listen. He could hear no sound of a man's breathing. The moon was behind a misty cloud. He waited as the cloud drifted, and the light grew stronger. Through the posts of the lean-to he could see the tumbled blankets of the bed. Garrick was gone.

He walked to the river, and stumbled against a skiff

drawn up in the willows. Garrick's skiff. Playing a hunch, he made a big circle around the entire mass of brush. His sense of smell, sharpened by the cool autumn night, detected the fresh odor of manure where a gully cut down through the banks. Again there was brief moonlight, and he read the sign of horses, no more than two hours old. He tracked them up the gully, an easy trail even at night, the hoofs deeply dug in friable white clay. Then, on the rim, it faded on the hard, grassy ground. Trailing would be impossible before daylight.

His eyes swept the rims, the gullies, river bottoms. He could see the roof of a shanty whitely shining in the moonlight. A dozen times he had ridden past, within a long stone's throw, without suspecting its existence, so well was it hidden among willows and box elders. It occupied a high bar of ground between the river and a shallow backwater that in flood seasons formed a side channel of the river. Something had disturbed the backwater, and moonlight made reflections on little bounding waves.

"Beaver," he muttered, but he knew it wasn't beaver. Those trappers working out from Sage Post had plucked the country clean.

The water became placid, but a shadow had come up along the bleached side of the shanty—the shadow of a man. It hesitated, and moved on. He heard a noise, a choked cry that could have been that of a prowling bobcat, a man, or simply in his own imagination.

He returned to the skiff, and pulled upstream hard against the current. He cleared a point. He was now less than a quarter-mile off. The oars in the locks made complaining noises. He stopped against the bank while muffling the locks with cloth torn from the bottoms of his homespuns, then he hunted quiet water, dipping easily. The water was only a foot or so deep, dimpled by slight cross-currents, and beyond lay the entrance to the backwater, a black tunnel bowered over by box elders and cottonwoods.

He laid one of the oars down, and used the other like a paddle. The skiff slid through broken moonlight into shadow. The entrance to the backwater narrowed to a scant ten feet; it was so shallow the skiff whispered against the muck bottom. Then he was inside, with nothing visible except a strip of starlit sky straight overhead. The blackness was baffling. It was the blackness of a mine a thousand feet underground. He could see nothing, not even the oar he held in his hands.

He paused, the oar slightly lifted. Water made a musical trickle from its blade. He kept pulling, just keeping the skiff in movement. Unexpectedly, with a slight shock, the boat went aground. To his left the brush had been chopped away, leaving only the new growth of that year. He could see the chimney end of the shanty shining in the moonlight.

He listened, but heard no one. He would have felt better if he had. He clambered to the prow, and got out, sinking halfway to his knees in muck. A myriad bubbles rose with a fermented smell. He groped, found a dead branch, and tied the mooring line. He waded on, with effort pulling his weight up from the sucking mud. Suddenly he realized that someone was straight in front of him, and he instinctively dived forward into foot-deep mud and water. As he fell, a gun exploded in his face.

It was so close the concussion hit him with a deafening, baffling impact. Powder scorched him across cheek and ear, but the bullet had missed. He crawled through muck and weeds, through dead brush, up a low bank. Men shouted in the darkness. Their voices seemed to come from all directions at once. He lurched to his feet. His clothing was tangled in the thorns. He ripped free and fell again, with guns whipping powder flame over him.

126

He rolled; he crawled; he drew his guns. The Navies were water-slick in his hands. He aimed upward at the gun flame, and pulled the triggers. His guns misfired with weak snaps. He thumbed and pulled again, with a like result. The powder was soaked, and only the percussion caps exploded.

He heard Robel's voice, and that of Tom Claus. There were others, too. The darkness around him was full of movement. He knew that they had been waiting for him, and that he had stepped off the skiff into an ambush.

Crawling through grass and low bushes, he heard hawk-faced Wally Claven cry: "Wolf, go get the skiff! He'll try to make it across the backwash."

John moved along, fending bushes from his face. They were spreading now, trying to cover every path of escape. He hurried, taking long strides, protected by the shadow of the brush. He collided with a man head on. It knocked both of them back. The man grunted and said something, and John knew it to be short, heavy-set Nick Bruce, one of the wagoners who had been throwing in with Robel.

John recovered himself first, and found Bruce still trying to get his balance, trying to move into the clear, through the bushes, and having a hard time because of the seepage hole filled with stagnant water behind him.

John said, "Stop, or I'll blow ye in half."

Nick drew in his breath sharply, surprised and frightened to learn John's identity. He took a step back, forgetting the hole. The earth crumbled, and he fell.

"Gar!" he bawled.

John lunged after him, carrying him back into the water.

Gar shouted: "Bruce? What is it?"

But John had thrust him under a foot of muck, weeds, and water. Nick lashed back and forth while John with knees and hands held him there.

Robel called again, "Bruce, what's wrong?"

Twisting, Bruce got free, and came up fighting for air. He tried to cry out for help, but only a high, wheezing sound came. He tried again, and John smashed him down with the barrel of his Navy.

Bruce lurched and went head foremost in the brush. He might have been stunned, or dead. Comanche John did not wait to see. He lunged across the seepage hole, over his knees in muck. He climbed slippery logs. He was again in the backwater. He waded hip-deep until he reached the other shore, but there he was stopped by cut-banks. The moon was emerging, and that made his plight worse. He had his choice of climbing the moon-bright clay bank or of skirting the narrow shore. He chose the latter. They saw him, and started to close in from both sides. A man, carrying a rifle, was clambering one of the steep banks to bushwack him from above.

John doubled back, waded the backwater again, and was almost in the place from which he had started. The skiff was there, but though he could see no one guarding it, he gave up the thought of using it. They would pick him off the instant he reached the river. He kept going. He found their horses tied among the box elder trees near the cabin. He chose one, a heavy-legged bay, and rode off, letting the animal find its way through bushes to a trail, and downriver toward the main camp.

"Leaky loads," he muttered, digging ball and powder charge from his Navies. "Poor grade o' bullet ball. I hope this is never found out about me. Jumped and chased, and never even fired a shot. What kind o' verse would *that* make for my song?"

CHAPTER SEVENTEEN

ROBEL AND HIS MEN were in their lean-tos, sleeping late when John got up, aching and ill tempered from the night before.

"You look like a fought-out tomcat," Prudence said with sour reproof when he came around for coffee and dough-god.

"I may be fought out, but I ain't been outfought."

"What you been up to?"

He parried the question. Food improved his spirits. "The thing I need is a woman's love and care. I'll be rich one o' these days, and if I had the right woman to guide me it's likely I'd end up being elected to Congress."

"If I had ye, the first thing I'd do is break ye of the to-baccy habit; next I'd break ye of loud talk and cursing; and then I'd break ye of shiftlessness; and then, so help me, I'd likely break your neck."

Buffalo Browers stood over him, big and grouchy, scouring his plate with sand and grass. "You sneak out of here every night, don't you? You got some varmint plan in your mind? Well, be careful; that's all I say. Those vigilantes are still in the country, so *be careful.*"

John started away without answering. He saw then that Tom Claus had come outside the lean-to, and was squinting against the sun.

"How about *them?*" he asked, pointing to Robel's camp. "Whar *they* sneak out to? How about your wage—that grubstake to put ye in the farming business? Ye collect that yet?"

He knew by the talk that Browers hadn't, and he knew

that there was dissatisfaction about wages. John slouched up the slight rise of ground, watching Claus and the shelters behind him. Apparently he was the only one up.

"Watch your step," Claus said. "I got no guns on. Kill me, you'll swing for it."

"When I got killing to do, I'll look for bigger game than you. I wouldn't want to kill you, nohow. It wouldn't be merciful to put all them lice out of house and home." He tried to see inside. "Whar's Bruce?"

"He's yonder."

John was relieved, because Bruce had a wife and children waiting for him in Deer Lodge.

When John turned away, Claus asked, "What did you want Bruce for?"

"I wanted to tell him that he'd tooken up with some low-ornery company."

Garrick had not returned. Comanche John saddled and rode back to the shanty where he had escaped ambush the night before. He found only the trampled ground and a few exploded percussion caps. He back-trailed the horses to Garrick's camp, but he found nothing there, either. When he returned, he saw the mackinaw boat lying quietly, the work of searching the river at a standstill. All the men were at camp, and the blacksmith, Vanderhoff, in his broken Dutch was making a speech. Ordinarily a speech by Vanderhoff would be the best sort of comedy, but today nobody was laughing.

"Moneys!" John could hear him say. "I vould see some moneys yet!"

Billy Harum, generally easygoing, elbowed Vanderhoff out of the way, and said: "Van is right. It's October. I say we'll have to be paid. If we're not paid, we'd better head for Hotsprings, and build shanties against the winter. Otherwise, where'll we be?" He waved a hand toward Robel's end of the camp. "When he sees he's not going to turn that treasure, you know what'll happen? He'll pull out, and we'll be stuck in these bottoms, a hundred miles from nowhere, at forty below zero, starving to death."

Buffalo Browers got up and advised them not to be hasty. He said that he was certain that Robel would keep his promise and pay off, cash money, and that he'd see him about it personally.

Then Vanderhoff started again, saying all the things he had said before. His tirade was interrupted when someone saw Gar Robel coming with his heavy, stiff-legged, stud-horse walk.

Gar spoke to each of the men in turn, grinned at Van, then asked him if he were running for Congress on the Whig ticket, and laughed loudly at his own joke. Then he waited for silence—and got it.

"Yeah, I know what the complaint is, and I don't blame you. Not a bit. You wanted a grubstake for winter, and here it is late fall, and no cabins, no money, no nothing. Well, you boys have shot square with me all the way, and I'll shoot square with you." He jerked a thumb at the mackinaw boat. "We'll close 'er down for the year. Oh, I'll stay on, me and some of my boys; but you have families to think of, so go ahead and break camp and get back to the Landing. Roll your wagons over to the Deer Lodge, or wherever your farms are, build your shelters, and get some venison frozen before the deep snow."

"How about our money?" Billy Harum called.

Robel drew out a book and a stub of pencil and began totaling. The group became very tense and still.

"It comes to better than $2,400. What do you want, gold or greenbacks?"

"Gold!" Vanderhoff cried. "Like so you said—"

"Right. Gold. But I don't make a practice of carrying that much in dust around with me." He snapped the book shut. "Break camp, get back to your wagons, and drive to the Landing. I'll cut over the hills to Bonanza, and put through a bank order for the gold. Then I'll come back and meet you."

It satisfied most of them, and the group broke up. John, still keeping watch, saw Robel engage Spotsy Huss and his wife in conversation, and afterward call on Buffalo Browers.

Later John had a chance to talk to Billy McCormick. "You heading for Bonanza, lad?"

Billy shook his head and winked. "Don't you think it would be an insult to the lass if I left?"

"What lass?"

"Mary Bird. Didn't you know? She's staying on."

John straightened, with his shoulders back and his thumbs hooked in his crossed gun belts.

Billy hurried to say: "Oh, now, 'tis nothing to take that posture about. She'll not be alone. Spotsy Huss and his woman are staying also, and later on Mary's people will come down for her."

"Who told ye they would?"

"It was his promise."

"Robel's?"

"The same."

John laughed roughly, with a jerk of his shoulders, and spat.

"Now, wait, man. It was she herself who wanted it."

"On account o' *you!*"

"Well, now, sure and I'd like to believe so—"

"How long do you think ye'll last once Robel has ye at his mercy?"

The young Irishman cried angrily, "I'm afraid o' no man!"

"I reckon the person that ain't just a little scared of Gar Robel is lacking in good sense, because, by grab, I'm leery of him myself."

"I doubt he is as black of heart as you say."

"Hold on! Why was it that Robel started his search *here,* and not a mile back along the river like everyone else? Why was he so sure the boat drifted past Brule when even the French trader wasn't? I'll tell ye why. Because he was here before. He was here when it burned, and he was here when the powder bar'l blowed. Yes, you're danged right; it was Robel and his gang that did it, and sunk it, and put the bullet in your uncle that caused his death."

"You have no right to say that!"

"They'd hang him in I-dee-ho. Yes, they would, Billy. He led the gang that slaughtered them all at that Eagletop."

He left Billy to hunt out Prudence Browers, who was working like a man, getting her belongings roped together in bundles for the packhorses.

"No, ye ain't," John said. "Ye ain't leaving her behind."

"Who?"

"You know who—Mary Bird."

She stopped, and stood erect. She had trouble meeting John's eyes. She kept looking past him, wiping a lock of graying red hair back from her forehead.

John said, "When I left her with ye—"

"I know, but try and tell *her* that." She raised her voice. "What the tarnation do you expect me to do, tie her hand and foot in a bundle, like those beddings, and toss her on a packhorse? Who are *you* to say what she should do, anyhow? You ain't her paw. You're just a road agent, wanted by every vigilance committee from hyar to Californy."

He muttered, "I took her away from him once, I guess I can take her away from him again."

"She won't go. I tried, and she won't go. She has her bonnet perched for the Irishman. Oh, she'll be all right. Billy will watch after her. Why, look at the size of him. He could whip his weight in wildcats, that one."

"How about polecats?"

Buffalo had come up. On his face was the same set truculence that always appeared when he laid his eyes on Comanche John.

"Where's Garrick?" Buffalo asked.

Comanche John looked him over. "I don't know. Why do ye ask me?"

"Somebody—I ain't saying who—but somebody saw you follow him downriver. He ain't been seen since."

John surprised Buffalo by saying: "Yes, I followed him. He had a camp thar. Did his doodlebugging from thar because you ignorant Pike's Peakers laughed at him. Practiced his Marlowe, too. For *me*, because I appreciated such. I'll lay gold agin greenbacks you never even *heered* o' Marlowe."

"That may be, but I heered of murder, and—"

"Hold on!" Prudence said. "Let's not start a ruckus." She asked John, "When'd you see him last?"

"It war last night, just past dark."

"Oh, thunder, he'll be around. I gave up trying to figure the coming and goings of that one. I known him to be gone for three nights at a stretch, then come in with a wild-eyed look and never say so much as skat to anybody." She shouted to her husband, "Why ye worried *now?*"

He muttered, "There's talk."

"Talk, talk. Talk's cheap. Talk's what you do with a breath when it's no good for anything else. Now lay a hand to that parcel, and be careful, because I got my good teacup in it."

Comanche John took care of his horse, making sure that none of the shoes had worn unevenly, and that none of his hoofs were split. The pony had been eating well of the long ripe buffalo grass in the bottoms. He was sleek, and of late he had shown a tendency to rear when the saddle was put on him; and that was just as well, for

Comanche John never knew when the time might come to ride some of the vinegar out of him. Usually he was satisfied to hobble the gunpowder, but this afternoon he staked him on a forty-foot rope, and hid his saddle in the sagebrush.

He saw gangling Beans Harum ride in bareback, beating the rump of his horse, and lead everyone in the upper end of camp away with him until not a soul was left to tell the rest what the trouble was. They waited until Beans and the men came back in sight, pulling something on a rude, three-pole travois. The crowd that had gathered closely fell away, and there was a sudden hush as Comanche John came up.

A man's body lay on the ground. He was not surprised to see that it was Justinn Garrick.

CHAPTER EIGHTEEN

GARRICK LOOKED small and disjointed. He was barefoot, and naked from the waist up. He was bruised and beaten, and the bottoms of his feet had been burned. And finally he had been killed by a bullet through the heart.

"You found him?" John said to Beans.

He nodded.

"Where?"

Beans was still scared. "By the bend. I was riding for horses. I seen something from way off. And there he was."

John knew that everyone's eyes were on him. He got rid of his tobacco so that he could talk better.

"He had a camp downriver. I visited him thar yesterday, at nightfall. He'd doodlebugged and found the gold.

135

Yes, he had. I saw a can of it, and felt it. B'sides, he told me so. Told me he was scared, and was going to git out of the country. Going to come back next summer with protection so's he'd be sure and git his share, and not maybe a bullet in the heart. But ye see, he didn't git out quite quick enough."

Buffalo Browers turned and looked him in the eye. He said, "You killed him!"

"Would I be here telling ye this if I kilt him? No, I'd be on the high lope."

His voice and words carried conviction, but Claven came walking among them, and said in his nasal, piercing tone:

"Wait! I don't think he would. That is Comanche John. He's the one who hid out on top of the jail in Whitebluff while the sheriff and a fifty-man posse combed every gulch and mining drift within ten miles. He's Comanche John who slept in the sheriff's bed in Yellowjack while that same sheriff prowled the town for him. Yes, and stole the sheriff's pants, and bragged about it afterward. Any *ordinary* man would kill and run. Not Comanche John. Comanche John will kill, and wait with the smoking gun still in his hand, and talk you out of it. He's made fools of other people. Now maybe he'll make fools of you—or maybe he won't. That's for you to say."

Billy McCormick cried, "I have heard no proof."

Buffalo shouted, "Ain't it proof enough that he's a known killer and road agent?"

"This is the Northwest. Haven't I heard it said that half the men here came two jumps ahead of a sheriff and one jump ahead of the Union draft?"

"He was at Garrick's camp!"

"It proves nothing. Myself or anyone might have tortured and murdered to learn the secret."

"I saw him!" came a voice from the edge of the crowd.

"Who said that?"

"I saw him!" It was Spotsy Huss, frightened and excited and as full of quick movement as a weasel. He had a gun, but he hadn't drawn it. He remained clear of Comanche John, keeping men between them. "Yes, I did! I saw him sneak out of camp right after breakfast this morning. I was suspicious of him. I've always been suspicious, right from the first day. Every man here knows it. We'd have turned him over to the vigilantes, and we'd have profited by the reward money long ago if—"

"We know all that!" Buffalo seized him by the shoulder and turned him, almost lifting his feet off the ground. *"What* about this morning? Did you follow him?"

"Yes! Yes, I did! I rode down this side of the river, and watched him. Garrick had a camp across there. I knew where it was—"

"Maybe *you* kilt him," John said.

"Let him talk," said Buffalo. "So he went there. What else did you see?"

Spotsy licked his lips. His eyes kept darting around, without resting on anything for so much as half a second. He said: "I know he did it. I know he did, that's all."

"How do you know?" Harum asked. "Maybe you just got a hunch he did, but a hunch isn't enough to hang a man."

"I tell you I know!"

"You see him?"

"I saw him bring the body across the river. Yes, he did! I saw that he had something in a skiff, but I couldn't tell what it was. I didn't want to ride over. I knew he'd kill me. Just like he's always wanted to kill me. So I rode up a draw, that draw right over there; you can see it; and I got off, and crawled up to the edge of the cutbank, and there he was carrying the body. He carried it up from the river. I saw him."

They had been watching Spotsy so intently that John had been able to fall back a step or two from the main mass of the crowd. He made no show of unholstering his Navies. But they were there in his hands when they looked at him.

"Yep, boys, these are my guns. Don't try anything. Thar's certain of ye it wouldn't bother my mind to kill, but the ones I'd *have* to kill would be a different matter. So keep your hands clear. It war a lie he told. It war the blackest kind of a lie. But he's of ye, he's one of your number, having come with ye from Kansas; and even *knowing* he's a liar you'd take his word before mine."

He retreated one step, then another, trying to watch all of them, feeling with his jack boots for the earth behind him.

Vanderhoff was trying to get out of sight. "No, Van! You're a blacksmith, not a gunman."

He watched Nick Bruce, squat, heavy-browed Nick Bruce, with whom he had struggled in the dark the night before; Bruce with a raw welt slanting into his hair in evidence of John's Navy barrel. And he watched Claven, who was stiffly erect, his hands raised. John backed another step. Harum had moved, and Bruce was partly hidden, but by the movement of his shoulder John knew he was lifting his gun from its holster.

"Harum!" he shouted.

Harum jumped at his name, and Bruce was there with the gun in his hand. He tried to fall away, to lift it, and fire, but John's right-hand Navy exploded, and the gun was smashed spinning in the air. Bruce fell from shock, rolled over, and lay clutching his hand.

"He ain't kilt," John drawled. "I'll tell ye why. Not because he don't deserve it, but because he's got a wife and young ones."

John kept backing slowly as smoke drifted up from

138

the Navy. Then he suddenly realized that their eyes were no longer focused directly on him. They were watching someone at his back. He started to turn, but he was jolted rigid by the hard ram of a gun in his spine.

"Drop 'em!" a voice said.

It was Gar Robel.

CHAPTER NINETEEN

ROBEL TOLD BROWERS to keep him covered, and returned his pistols to their holsters. He seemed well satisfied with himself. Standing with his shoulders reared back, he looked taller than his six feet one, heavier than his 190 pounds. Today he carried all his weapons—at each hip a double pistol loaded with buckshot; in an armpit holster the Wells Fargo model Colt, and in its sheath the heavy, old-fashioned Green River trapper's knife. There was just a trace of a smile on his lips as he looked at Comanche John. Then that faded, and his caribou face settled into its usual heavy, truculent lines.

"Hang him, hang him," men were saying.

Gar said: "Yes, that's something we should have done long ago, and poor Garrick would be alive today. I say string him up; the sooner the better."

Spotsy picked up the cry, "Hang him!"

"Where's some rope?" shouted Bruce.

"Piece of line in the rowboat."

"Beans, go fetch the line."

"Beans!" It was his father, Billy Harum. Beans stopped, and looked at him. "You stay out of this."

Robel said with side-of-the-mouth contempt: "What's wrong with you, Harum? You going soft?"

"I'm not letting the boy get mixed in any hanging, that's all."

Spotsy said, "I'll fetch the rope."

But someone had already gone for it.

The rope was frayed, with some of its strands unwound, and it was wet from the river.

"That'll never do," Buffalo said.

"Why?"

"It won't hold him. He's heavy. Man's weight hits the end of a rope, and—"

"We can try, can't we?"

"And drop him a second time? Listen, he may be a killer and a road agent, but I say a man deserves a strong rope and a good drop no matter what he is."

Robel said: "Sellers, get that rope off the grapple. You can bet that will hold him!"

Sellers came up dragging it. It was an inch in diameter, stiff and wet, and he kept bending it in his hands, trying to limber it up for the knot.

Comanche John had watched all this with droopy-eyed, expert appraisal. He said: "I'm glad to see you and your boys have tooken things over, Gar, because I know this is something you're practiced in. For instance, thar was that prospector at Cement Gulch that ye hung so your partners could jump his claim. That was a good piece of business, and should have netted ye a neat penny. Too bad ye blew it all in on likker and gambling, or it wouldn't be—"

"I might blow your head off so hanging wouldn't be necessary."

"Now, a man shouldn't be ashamed of his past. He ought to git up, and admit it all, like I did when I hit the sawdust trail. Tell 'em about the Placerville fire, too, and about that Eagletop—"

Robel took a long stride, and hit him backhand with a snapping swing and pivot of his rawboned body. The sound of it, a solid *whop!* across Comanche John's cheek and jaw, could be heard through the length of the camp. It knocked John to a sitting position. He hoped to fall within reach of his Navies, but the blow had a merciless, stunning force. He sat with his legs bent under him, trying to shake it off. He got to one knee. Each move sent a new wave of dizziness across his brain.

He heard Prudence shout, "I don't like that!" She was coming toward them, holding her calico dress up from the cactus.

"Keep back, woman!" her husband said.

"You mean you'd let him manhandle somebody whilst you held a gun at his back? What kind of a man be ye? That kind of a man ties up a horse and beats him."

Spotsy cried: "He ain't as good as a horse. He's just a murdering—"

"Git out o' my way."

When Spotsy failed to move, she seized him by the front of his shirt and shook him. She shook him like a hound shaking a rabbit. His head snapped and his hat flew off. His shirt came loose from his pants, and his long reddish hair was strung over his face. He tried to defend himself, and swung at her; but she was larger than he, and she held him at arm's length so that he could not reach her.

"Git a stick, Spotsy!" somebody cried.

"Keep your mouth shut!" Prudence said.

She held Spotsy with one hand and whopped him with the other. "Take that, ye sneaking wretch! And that! I'm sick of you and your yellow spite. You're a liar, and you're a cheat, and I have a pretty good idee that it's you that's been stealin' my hard sugar."

Her husband was bellowing, "Woman, git back to your cooking!" but she did not hear him.

She had Spotsy in retreat, and she kept him going. With a final thrust she drove him away from her. For a moment he kept his feet. He back-peddled desperately for a dozen steps, waving his arms for balance, but his momentum outraced his legs and he sat down abruptly. There was a cottonwood stump behind him. His head snapped and struck it. It left him sag-mouthed, with his eyes out of focus.

Prudence huffed and blew. She had long wanted to whop Spotsy, and now she felt better.

Her husband finally gained her attention. "You hear me? Get back to the wagon!" When she started to answer, he bellowed in her face: "Yes, git back! I've taken a lot from you, meddling in a man's affairs, but this is the end. You get back to your packing, or by the gawds I'll drag you there."

She met his eyes, and realized that he meant it.

"You hang the wrong man, Mr. Browers, and it'll be on your soul, not mine."

"*Let* it be! I don't like hanging any better'n the next one, but sometimes it has to be done."

Comanche John said, "I don't guess you God-fearing Missouri and Kansas folk would hang a man without a trial."

She said, "How about *that*, Mr. Browers?"

"I ain't agin trials. We got time. We'll give him one. Then he won't be able to say he ain't been hung first-class."

Robel was between them. "Trial, you idiot? What in hell's got into you—"

"I'm still running my outfit, and there's more of us than there are of you. I say we give him a good fair, impartial trial, and hang him afterward."

CHAPTER TWENTY

DARKNESS HAD COME EARLY, with wind that kicked dust eddies along the trampled ground. It was a cold wind, with a feel more of snow than of rain, from a bullet-colored sky. A fire had been built, a big fire of driftwood logs that lighted the bottoms from the river to the cutbank, and men were glad to gather around and feel its heat.

Comanche John, with hands tied behind him, sat cross-legged, chewing and arching tobacco juice at the fire. At one side had been set a puncheon bench for the jurors. At the other was an empty barrel for the judge. Across the fire, together with most of Garrick's belongings, were John's Navies on their wide belts which even on the ground retained the shape of his body.

Buffalo Browers, who had changed to a fresh linsey shirt and trimmed his whiskers for the occasion, trod up and thumped on the barrel with the butt of his six-shooter, asking for order. "Hear ye, the co't is now in session." He had already made his decision about jurors, but he pretended to be pondering it as he looked around at the rough, bewhiskered, heavy-booted men. "McFadden, you be foreman. Harum, take you. And you, Billy, and you, Van. And Stevens. And Sellers, I guess you."

"I object," said Comanche John.

Black Dave said, "You object to being here at all, don't you?" and everybody laughed.

Robel said, "Name one more so we can have a majority."

John said, "Hanging is done only on unanimous ver-

143

dict; that's according to Blackstone."

"To hell with Blackstone. Name one more."

"I'll break the tie," Browers said, "if there is one." He cleared his throat. He waited for the right degree of attention. "Boys, a man was killed. Not only was he killed, but there was good enough evidence he·was tortured. All in all, it was about as low down as I ever see, and we're here to hang the guilty party."

"Providing it's me," John said. He chuckled and arched a long spurt at the fire. It hit and sizzled. With hands tied, he tried to wipe his lips with an upward twist of his shoulder. "Now, the next thing ye do is call on the persecution. I don't care who that be, but I know who I want for *my* lawyer. I want Tom Claus. Yep, Tom, the dirtiest, drunkenest, lousiest, ignorantest man that ever come up the gold trail from Californy. Ask me why? I'll tell ye. I never was a man to go halfway. If I can't have the best, then I want the worst, and Tom will be the worst lawyer that a man ever had."

Claus giggled and hiccuped. He had just finished the residue of his chokecherry cordial which he had fermented in a hollowed-out log. He was a trifle unsteady. He was gangling and slovenly. He had long, unkempt grayish hair and whiskers. According to his own brag, he had last bathed when he was shipwrecked on the Sacramento River in the year of Fifty-three. His clothing, almost entirely of buckskin, was black and slick from grease. He carried a brace of Navy pistols low on his thighs, with the butts pointed the wrong way so that he had to twist his hands around to draw; but those who had seen him in action said he performed it with considerable swiftness.

Some of the men started hee-hawing and calling: "Defend him, Claus! Make a speech."

He came forward. "What am I supposed to do?"

"Your client," said Sellers. "Plead his case."

"Waal, I plead guilty. I plead he git hung."

Prudence charged in and cried: "This is goin' to stop. It's sacrilegious. You're making a joke of life and death."

Her husband said, "He asked for it."

John hopped to his feet. He did a bent-over polka step. With hands tied behind him, the dance looked more like something he had learned from the Sioux. He said: "Don't pay her no heed, Claus. You go right ahead. Make a speech for me. You're doing top rate."

Claus, half drunk, and for once the center of things, said, "What's more, I plead that this low-down skunk I'm defendin' be hung with a rough rope."

"Yipee!" said John. "Give me both bar'ls. Tell 'em how I got cemeteries named after me all the way from Pike country across the Plains. Tell 'em how I was raised by the coyotes to howl like a wolf. I was, for a fact. I'm a ring-tailed ripper from the Rawhide Mountains, and if ye set still and listen I'll teach ye the language of the timber wolves. *Ya-hoo-o!*"

"Stop it!" cried Prudence. "Stop it, I say. Ain't ye any decency? Ain't you got any respect for the dyin', even if it is yourself?"

He got away from her. In doing so, he stumbled over the fire. He burned one foot and hopped on the other. He could not keep his balance with his hands tied, and he slipped to the ground. He landed in a seated position, with his boots out and his elbows and his tied hands behind him. By apparent accident he had knocked some burning sticks from the fire, and he had fallen with one just below his hands. Guided by its heat, he slid himself back a few inches at a time, until the burning stick touched a forearm with sudden pain. He endured it with clenched teeth. He moved, but only a little. His wrists were bound by wrappings of small rope. Like all the other rope in camp, it was damp from immersion in the river. It made a slight hiss against the coal. It dried and commenced to scorch. It still burned his wrists. He pulled the rope taut to keep the coal farther away. A raw scorched odor came to his nostrils. It became stronger. It seemed impossible that someone would not notice, but Prudence was ripping into Tom Claus, telling him his shortcomings, and he had ceased to take it in good spirit.

"Browers," he said, "you keep this woman of yours away from me, or by the Gawd I'll forgit I'm a gent'man and shoot her. I will. I'll shoot her. A man can take just so much, and I've tooken it."

Robel was there to step in. "You're drunk, sit down."

"I'm not drunk. I'm—" Then he realized who was talking to him, and with a surly lift and drop of his shoulders he slouched away.

"That was a good plea," Comanche John said. Smoke from the rope spread across his back, through the stiff autumn grass, and rose in a thin fog around his arms and shoulders, but no one noticed. "You figger up, Claus, and send me a bill for your fees."

"Whar to? To Hades?"

"You'll not see *me* growing horns." He twisted his knuckles together, hard. The coal was burning his wrists like the fires of the hell they talked about. He kept talking as sweat grew in droplets on his cheeks. "Wings, by grab. Can't ye see me with wings and a harp? None of your jew's harps, neither. A real gold and mother-of-pearl harp like I seen in the dance halls in San Francisco."

"Somebody's clothes is on fire," McFadden said.

People looked themselves over.

McFadden said: "I tell you I smell cloth burnin'."

"All this talk o' hell," said John.

The damp rope gave out volumes of smoke, and the stench grew stronger.

"Ain't me," said Claus.

"Something fell in the fire."

He twisted his wrists. One of the weakened strands frayed out. There was a tiny ripping sound as it parted. He was able to work his right hand free. The rope remained in loose coils on his left wrist. He kept it that way. He was on one knee, his wrists still pressed together. He did not let his eyes wander to the guns, but he knew exactly where they lay, how many steps it would take to reach them, where his next move would take him, and his next.

He suddenly jumped to his feet, crying, "That's *me* on fire!"

Several started to laugh, but they were cut short by a warning shout from Black Dave:

"Hey! He's loose. He's making for the guns!"

He dived headlong. Somebody fired a blast from a shotgun. The charge roared past him, tore the earth, glanced upward among the legs of the jurors. There was a mad stampede to get out of the line of fire. Men screamed from pain, and men cursed. John was on his face, in the momentary protection of Garrick's luggage, and he had his guns. He didn't try to strap them on. He didn't even try to draw them from their holsters. He dived again, rolled over, was on his feet for two leaping steps, and then went down again beyond a pile of firewood. He had one Navy drawn. He fired twice along the ground, through the fire, scattering sparks and charred wood, adding for a moment to the turmoil.

"Git down or git kilt!" he roared. "I been a long time without action, and nothing I'd rather have than live targets."

They fired at his voice. He kept going, through trampled sage, around bundles ready for packhorses, along a little dry gully. Chadwaller's dog, unable to resist the sight of a fleeing man, was after him, but he turned and ran howling when a slug from John's left-hand Navy ripped the sod between his front feet.

John stopped and shouted, "Hyar I am. Come and git me!"

He was answered by a swarm of bullets. He turned up a steep-sided gully, knowing they would see him, wanting them to see him. Then he dropped to his knees and crawled back. A bullet struck the clay bank high over him, and whistled away, leaving a puff of dust. There were more bullets, wilder bullets. He was on his feet now, with his guns belted. He walked, because running wasn't his style. He came up to Robel's lean-to, and stopped long enough to help himself to powder and ball. He even stood for a time, freshening his chew and watching with droopy-eyed interest the progress of the search as they spread out with an idea of cornering him in the gully. They weren't trying too hard, and he chuckled. Plenty of whoop and holler, but none of them wanted to be the man who came up against Comanche John in the dark.

His pony was waiting, picket string tight, head up.

"Ye hear that gunfire? Means only one thing: farewell to the Yallerstone."

CHAPTER TWENTY-ONE

COMANCHE JOHN DID NOT TAKE the chance of building a fire. He slept as best he could, without blankets, in a brush-choked gully, awaking every half-hour to beat the creeping chill out of his body. With the first gray of dawn, he was back in the saddle.

He considered riding to Alder, and to Last Chance. He thought it over while examining his heat-blistered wrists, and opening the blisters with his bowie. He came to no decision. The sun rose, and grew hot, and he became acutely aware of hunger.

Ducks were in from the north, darkening the surface of a slough. He shot one, a fat mallard, and roasted it on a prop stick, over a bed of coals. He had no salt, so he ate it Indian style, with handfuls of frost-sweetened choke-cherries for dessert. It felt good to be on the loose, living off the country, and he had a good notion to chuck it all, camp life and city life, and go Indian. He thought of all the squaws he had seen that summer in the Kutenai country, mentally taking his pick of them. Then his hand happened to go to his pocket where the pinch of gold dust still lay. As he hefted it in his fingers, he knew that he would never rest easy in a teepee, and that gold fever was something a man never got out of his blood.

He got up, tramped out his fire, and rode the rims, keeping watch on the river. He watched for Robel's men, but he saw not a soul. The day passed, the sun set, the moon rose, and he watched by moonlight.

"Gold," he muttered. "Gold by the bucketful, gold by the ton. Yaller gold, and all of it Robel's."

Sheltered among box elders, his fire hidden by a pocket in the coulees, John roasted another mallard. He was half through his meal, slicing dark breast meat and carrying it into his mouth with his bowie, when he knew by the head-up movement of his horse that someone was coming. He stood with a hand on the halter as steps whispered up through the autumn covering of dead leaves, and he recognized the tall, erect shape of Billy McCormick.

John said, "Evening, lad," and laughed when Billy jumped as if he'd been touched by a hot iron. "You'd get kilt around some camps, sneaking up like that. But long as you're here, pull up some ground and set, and I'll serve ye my specialty, duck à la Blackfeet, without salt. It's fine when ye get onto it." Then he asked, "How'd ye know whar to find me?"

"It's an instinct I have for human nature."

"How is it in camp? Those Pike's Peakers of Browers's leave yet?"

"Tomorrow, or maybe day after."

"Mary still figure to stay behind?"

"Aye, she is that, with Mrs. Huss." And he cried, anticipating John's objection, "But I'll be on hand to see that no harm comes to her!"

"Think you're a match for Robel? Well, maybe. But look in your bed for rattlesnakes. He'll kill you, or any man, rather than cut a share of that treasure."

"And what will I be doing all the time?"

"Waal, right now you're going yonder with me for a talk with the only one in that ignorant emigrant camp with any common sense—Prudence Browers!"

Two huge campfires still burned at the camp, lighting the breadth of Brule Bottoms. Supplies were being packed into bundles, and the bundles torn apart and repacked when they failed to pass the inspection of Buffalo Browers. Even at half a mile, from atop the rims, they could hear him bellow: "Git the lump out of that. Whar'd you learn to load a packhorse? And that one's too big. How many times I tell you they got to balance off, equal on both sides? Want your packsaddle to end up beneath the horse's belly?"

The men were tired, and cursed back at him. Bundles had been stacked in a heap near the cook shanty. Horses, after weeks of roaming the bottoms, were waiting, held by a rope corral. Finally things quieted somewhat; the final bundle met Buffalo's approval, and after whanging a tin pan, Mrs. Huss called them in her thin voice for a cup of tea.

Soon the fires died, the camp quieted.

"They hit the shucks, Billy," Comanche John said. "Better we git our visiting done."

" 'Tis a grave risk, riding down there, what with the reward Spotsy could collect, and bands of hangmen roaming the country."

"By grab, when I think of what I'm worth in ree-ward money, here and in I-dee-ho, and in Californy, too, I'm tempted to surrender so's I can collect it myself. Worth my weight in gold, mighty near, if ye figured it all up; and that's no mean accomplishment for a man without eddication, brung up on spoonbread and catfish in a shanty so deep in the bottoms even the hawgs had the shakes. Did you know I was brung up in the country o' Pike, just across the river from that town o' New Salem, Illinois, whar Abe Lincoln got his start?"

The trail led them to the cutbank. It was dark, so they trusted to their horses. The path ended. They slid the final ten feet, raising clouds of clay dust that were invisible in the darkness, but filled their lungs and nostrils nevertheless. The descent had made noise, and now they stopped to listen.

John said: "I've thought about it considerable, and it *does* seem peculiar, two famous men like Abe and me, getting started out in life so close together. Billy, I wouldn't want it to git out that I said this, but down inside I always had a admiration for that cussed Lincoln. Look whar he started, and now the whole country's talking about him. Real likable lad, from all I heered. Just got off on the wrong foot. Got to the city, whale-oil lights, bad companions. Took to associating with gamblers, abolitionists, and lawyers and the like. Gave him cee-gars, I suppose, and flattered him. Got so he couldn't tell right from wrong. So blinded he couldn't see that the South had every privilege to go her merry way. Stubborn. Had to be taught. Had to have old Robbie Lee teach him a lesson. It's sad, though, when ye think what he *could* have done."

Chadwaller's brindle dog got scent of them, and came baying, but he stopped and tried to throw his rear end out of joint with wagging when he learned who it was.

Billy, more nervous than ever, whispered: "It is madness for you to come here. Mrs. Browers holds no charity for you. She names it an evil day that you first showed your face."

"Women talk that way, but I'll wager if she was a widda I couldn't rid myself of her this side of a church."

A grease-dip lamp was burning with a sputtery orange flame, lighting the inside of Black Dave's lean-to, and they could see the shadows of men, their slight changes of position in turning cards and betting. The usual game was in progress.

"Gambling it away," John muttered, "before even it's raised from the river."

"Here it is," whispered Billy, and dismounted beside a long, low dugout-shanty.

Inside, someone snored and snorted.

"Listen to him!" John said. "That Buffalo Browers! How's she put up with him? The more I think of it—"

"Hush!" said Billy.

Stiff, untanned buffalo hides had been pegged along the arch log to make doors. As Billy hushed him, one of the hides swung inward, and Mary Bird was there, peering out at them.

"Ye wake easy," said John, and Billy hushed him again.

He guessed then that she had been awake all the time, and that she knew Billy had left camp, and was worrying about him. Perhaps she was relieved, but nothing showed in her face, which was perfectly composed and expressionless, except for what one could read in her large dark eyes.

"Call Prudence," said Billy.

She disappeared, and a second later the snoring stopped.

Prudence said something, and emerged, pulling an old blanket cape around her, the horse pistol in her hand.

"Why, Prudence," said John, "ye snore!"

"I do not snore, and I'd like to know what business it is of yours if I did." She had the pistol ready and cocked, but she did not aim it. "What in the thunder are you doing here? Ain't you satisfied getting away with your neck?"

"No," said John, "I ain't."

"We put up with you long enough. Now, if you got any mistaken idees about—"

"I didn't kill that actor, and ye know it."

Prudence muttered and grumbled, and 'lowed it didn't differ what you hung a road agent for so long as you hung him.

John said: "Hearken to these words. I'm as innocent as a babe unborn. Except for one sheebang run by a varmint, and maybe one no-account Wells Fargo coach, I been true to that vow I made when I got religion twice twelvemonth ago. I have, Prudence. I been pouring ile in my lamp, and when I turn up my toes, with my boots all blackened and sitting beside the bed, it'll shine bright and clear, because it gladdens the angels to pluck a drifter up from the black gulch o' sin, it does for a certainty."

"Wa-al," she said, "I dunno. I dunno about you, John. You talk converted, but it seems to me you're always getting set to act like a varmint."

"I want my share of the gold, that's all."

She grabbed him by the front of his buckskin vest, and he felt for a second the strength that had rendered Spotsy helpless.

"You mean he *did* find the gold?"

"O' course. *Garrick* did. 'Tree by the waters of Babylon.' Marlowe. That's all I learnt from him. But Gar tor-

153

tured him, kilt him. Why else did he come straight here and say, 'Break camp, git yourselves over to the Deer Lodge'?"

She grumbled, without conviction: "Waren't our gold anyhow. We be just working for wage."

"Maybe. But Gar has seen how people act around that much gold, and he wanted ye away. Got rid of Garrick first, then me, next you and yours, then Billy, I'll wager. See how it goes? Spotsy and Bruce think they're smart, staying behind. I'd hate to be in their boots once Gar has no more use for 'em. By grab, I'd hate even to be in Claven's or Dirty Tom's boots once that time comes, because Gar's like one o' them old-time pie-rats that buried the swag and then kilt off all his men that knew whar it was."

Mary Bird moved suddenly and whispered a warning, and an instant later John realized that Buffalo had awakened.

He was in the opening, holding Mary aside with one hand, his sawed-off shotgun in the other.

Prudence said, "Mr. Browers, what's the meaning of this?"

"You ask me what—"

"Unhand that child and put the gun down."

John said: "Never mind. I got him centered right betwixt the eyes. Don't you worry about losing him, because I know whar I can find ye a better one."

Prudence got between the men, telling them to put their guns down. Then she said to her husband, "There's talk that the gold's been found."

It made his body jerk erect. "Who said?"

"Me," said John. "I seen it with my own eyes. I felt it with my hands. I listened to it jingle from one hand to another. I hefted a can of it, heavier'n a can of lead."

"Where is it?"

"Why, come to think, hyar's a sample," and John drew

the pinch of nuggets and coarse stuff from his pocket. He shook it in the hollow of his palm beneath Browers's nose, and chuckled at the pop-eyed look on his face. "Yep, yaller gold. Look at 'er shine, even without light. Like foxfire."

"You know where the treasure is, then?"

"No, but Robel does. Learnt from Garrick. That's why Garrick died. That's why he wants me and you and all of us out of the country."

"I don't believe it!"

But he *did* believe it. His eyes, following the gold all the way back to John's pocket, showed that he believed it.

John said, "Gold by the sackful, gold by the wheelbar'ful. Gold more'n enough for any one man, or any ten men. All ye could carry. How'd ye like that, Buffaler?"

Prudence said, "We don't have a share coming."

"Hell, Maw—"

John said, "*I* got one coming, and Garrick had one, and Billy. And we don't feel about it like Gar Robel. Share and share alike, that's our motto."

CHAPTER TWENTY-TWO

COMMANDED BY BUFFALO BROWERS, the emigrants broke camp in the morning, and with laden packhorses started the heavy job of moving supplies back to the wagons that waited at Sage Creek. Everything went smoothly, and by sundown that first night they were completely out of Brule Bottoms, at a temporary camp on Wolf Creek Coulee, fourteen miles away.

Robel was now free to move toward recovering the treasure, and it had been the hope of Browers and Comanche John that he would proceed immediately to the spot where it was located. They waited, on horseback, on a hill above the camp until long past midnight, but there was no unusual activity; no one, so far as they could see, had left camp.

At last Billy McCormick crept up and found them.

"They'll not make any move tonight," he said. "Not with all of them drunk on that new batch of chokecherry wine."

"You better stay and keep an eye on Mary Bird," John said.

"She's sitting with Mrs. Huss. Mrs. Huss took sick tonight, I think at the thought of being left behind."

John muttered: "Ought to shoot him. Keeping a woman thar, agin her will."

"She didn't say anything, or we'd of took her!" Buffalo said defensively.

Billy McCormick had a chew of tobacco with them, and made ready to return. "Get some sleep for yourselves," he said from down the hill. "They'll not lead you to it tonight."

The moon was covered by a thin haze, and a wind sprang up, bending the stiff stalks of buffalo grass, making the men turn their backs and pull their jackets around their necks.

"I seen it blizzard here in October," John said. "Year of Fifty-five, and I'd been to Hangtown, first place they turned the color in all the Territory of Montana, only it war called I-dee-ho then, or Dakotah. Snow above the fetlock, and eighteen below. In *October*. You're too late for shanties this year, Browers. Best ye pitch camp at Yellowstone Landing. After *this*, o' course."

They hunted a draw where the wind was less. There was no moon now, and snow was coming in little hard pellets. They kept going, and stopped at the river's edge about a mile below Brule.

"What now?" Browers asked.

"Playing a hunch." He pointed across the dark water. "Across thar. Backwater trapper's shanty. Might have left some of the boys at Brule to drink wine and carry on just to fool folks. Gar is tricky. A man has to git up at thirteen o'clock if he expects to outwit Gar. Let's have a look."

"Cross the river *tonight?*"

John chuckled, "Cold bath's good for the muscles. Toughens ye."

They crossed, naked, with their clothes and guns on the saddle, hanging to the tails of their swimming horses. The river felt warm after the wintry air, but it was chilling on the shore, trying to dry and get dressed.

The shanty was deserted, but it still held an odor of tobacco smoke, and outside was a boot track in a wind-blown accumulation of snow.

"Sneaked off under our noses!" John said, and cursed. "But let's try our luck downriver. It's black as a gambler's heart, but you can't tell, they might have a lantern showing."

No lantern showed, but it was lighter because of the snow which had gathered here and there on the windward sides of grass clumps. They found horse tracks, lost them, found them again, and then lost them altogether in a brush-filled coulee.

"Headed for the river," John said.

The river was empty, like gray metal under the gray-dark sky. The flats and the hills bounding it were devoid of life. Day commenced to break.

"Think they went to it?"

"Not on horseback."

Browers's voice showed alarm. "Why they want to lead us here?"

"Getting itchy between the shoulders? Well, maybe it

is ambush. When ye go out looking for gold, that's the chance ye got to take."

They remained hidden; daylight came slowly and dissolved the heavy shadows; and when there was still no show of life they ventured out across the bottoms. They found the tracks again, now doubling back toward Brule.

"Gone," John said. "They was made hours ago, before we even left the shanty. Look at that print. That's that big bay gelding of Gar's, shod with half-round."

"I don't like it out here, in plain view, daylight. If they come—"

"Then git out. Go home with your old woman."

He blew back, "I got as much nerve as you have!"

They rode downriver side by side, Browers with his jaw squarely set, but with eyes that showed his nervousness, hunting the rims to his left and the brush to his right. It was warmer now; the sun was out briefly, and only little streaks of dampness showed where the snow had drifted the night before.

"Hid their skiff," John drawled, shooting tobacco juice.

"I see nothing."

"They drug it. Skiff pretty heavy. Weighed 250, 300 pound. Too much for two men. See those streaks in the mud?"

The skiff, as John had guessed, was pulled up in the willows. Its skid marks led to the water's edge, but the river left no trail, and stretched beyond, wide and shallow and featureless.

"Now where?" Buffalo demanded, showing plainly that he considered this dead end to be Comanche John's fault.

"Yonder." He slouched in the saddle, resting his left knee around the horn. He chewed, regarding the river from beneath his slouch hat. He regarded it for a long time.

It was still shallow, despite the slight autumn rise. In

mid-stream he could see the deviation of current and chop waves that indicated a sandbar. Yonder, a cottonwood driftlog had come to rest, and lay with roots like gnarled fingers pointing against the current. Still farther was another mudbar, or at least a shallow spot, because he could count six seedling willows or cottonwoods growing in a perfect row about three feet out of the water. On shore nearly all the leaves had fallen, but the frost had not touched so strongly there, close to the river's surface, and the saplings held theirs, yellowed, but still with enough elasticity to flutter in the breeze.

"A tree," he said. "A tree of gold by the waters of Babylon."

"What?"

"Ain't ye up on your Marlowe?"

"Marlowe who?"

"Marlowe, ye ignorant Pike's Peaker, and a real ripsnorter of a poet if thar ever was one. I know Marlowe frontwards and backwards, and sometime I'll teach ye a verse or two of him so's ye can go around and make folks think ye wasn't brung up with the hawgs out on the bottoms. But right now I ain't got the time."

He dismounted, telling Browers to mind the horses. He checked the skiff. It contained a pikepole, a grapple, and an old section of stove grate for an anchor, all wet and muddy from the river. And in the inch or so of bilge floated a cottonwood leaf still yellow-green.

"The tree o' gold," he muttered, picking up the leaf. "Tree o' gold by the waters o' Babylon."

He slid the skiff down to the water. With the current favoring him, it took only three or four minutes to reach the straight row of saplings. They were higher than he had supposed, about five feet above the water. Peculiarly, there seemed to be no sandbar for them to take root. They just grew there, jiggling slightly from the current flowing around them. He swung the boat and dropped the anchor. It caught solidly, stopping him with a jerk. He knew then that the mackinaw boat had sunk there, that her green cottonwood ribs had sprouted shoots, and that those shoots were the saplings he had seen from shore.

He stripped off his clothes, folded them, placed them in a pile on the seat, with his guns and powder flask on top. In his excitement he had forgotten about the possibility of danger from shore, but he remembered now, and forced himself to look, and look long, both ways along the river. Nothing. Not even a sign to show where Buffalo Browers and the horses waited, hidden in willow brush. The sun had disappeared, and rain mixed with fog blew around him. It struck his naked body in icy gusts, but even that did not bother him.

He shivered, more from excitement than from cold, and kept saying, "The tree o' gold," under his breath, through his teeth, over and over, making it into a song, singing it in a whisper to the tune of an old revival hymn:

"It growed thar by the water, the water, the water:
It growed thar by the waters o' Bab-y-lon."

He groped over the side with the pikepole. The wreck lay about four feet down, invisible in the roily water. He lowered himself over the side, got his feet on the old deck, and stood chest-deep.

The wrecked mackinaw boat had come to rest at a list of about twenty degrees, and he had to use the pikepole to keep his balance as he groped along, feeling with his bare feet. He located the prow, and worked his way back. He struck something with his thigh. It was a post set upright, apparently as a guide. He went under the water, one arm around the post, the other groping down through a hole in the hull. The hole did not go all the way through. The mackinaw boat had been built double-bottomed, with a six- or eight-inch space between, and the hole where the post was wedged went through the upper layer of planks only.

He came up for air, filled deeply, and went down again, this time reaching far beneath the false bottom. He found buckskin sacks, packed tightly, slick as fish from long soaking. He got a grip on one and, using all his strength, pulled it out. Its weight made him stagger. He lost the pikepole. He was under the water, carried by the current, but he kept hold of the gold, and its weight kept him from sliding clear of the boat. He got a slippery foothold, crawled, and made a lucky grab at one of the saplings. He came up blowing water, but with the gold. Still clinging to the sack, he managed to make the boat and dump it over the side.

He wanted to open it, naked as he was, with river water streaking from his hair and whiskers, and the storm licking around him. But he got hold of himself, talking aloud.

"No, John. That's how ye git kilt, looking at loot when ye should be looking for hangmen."

It was the second time in twelve hours that he had been in the river. His clothes were still damp. He crouched in the boat, shivering, stripped water from his body, used his old green silk neckerchief for a towel. Dressed once more, rowing against the current made him warm again.

Browers forgot his caution, and rode down the bank to meet him, "What'd you find?"

"Gold."

"You did then! You did!"

"Now, don't go wild and skeer the fish. I brought a bag of it, and—"

"Just one? There's more—"

"O' course thar's more, but it's a hard lift out o' deep water, with poor footing. A man go down in that current, he mightn't come up before spring."

"Let me see it, let me see—"

"Keep your hands away from thar or ye'll git 'em shot off." Browers straightened and looked at John with his mouth agape. "Yes, I mean it. Lend your weight. We'll skid this boat back whar we found it." He looked around at the ground. "No, those skid tracks don't matter, it's these—our horses. You gather up that fresh sign, and throw it in the river. We'll pour water over the tracks, make 'em look old."

He tied the bag of gold to his saddle. He sat against it, for he liked the feel of it, even though water kept oozing from the sack, soaking his thighs through his homespun pants. A thought struck him, and he rode on up a clean-swept area that had been part of the river bed during the high water of June. It had occurred to him that *that* had been a part of the river bed when the boat had sunk the year before.

The high water of repeated springs had left its mark with deposits of sand and gravel. As he had expected, there was the whitish rock. Erosion had smoothed it in most places, but at one spot he could see where a piece had been broken out. He knew that it was the very piece that had been treasured in Dakotah's parfleche. Of all the strata he had seen, only this lay above high-water mark; of all the strata only this one had been visible along the north bank when Dakotah had swum ashore.

"Should o' found it," he muttered. "Should have found it before Garrick."

He went back to where Buffalo was still sweating up from the river, dumping hatfuls of water over the horse tracks.

"That'll do. Be careful, don't put your footprint down in that wet. You got a bigger bootprint than Robel, and he'd know. Like I said, ye got to git up at thirteen o'clock when ye fool that lobo."

Buffalo cried, "We're not just leaving with only this one bag o'—"

"That's a long job. All-day job. They see us, and we wouldn't be two rich men heading for the bright lights of San Francisco. We'd be two dead men drifting down the river to ol' Missou."

CHAPTER TWENTY-THREE

THEY MADE A WIDE CIRCLE to avoid the old camp, and came back to the river at Rocky Point, the two-thirds mark on the journey to Sage.

It was dark when they got there, the camp a clutter of supplies, wet and cold and miserable. With no dry wood, Prudence's cookfire was a smudge that had already laid a fog of blue smoke over everything.

"There's no heat in *that* fire," said Buffalo, getting off and trying to warm his back, "and here I am, still wet from the river."

She shouted, "Well, why warn't you here to build one?" She lowered her voice, "First duty is to these folk that elected you cap'n, and not chasing around, searching for gold. Come back empty-handed, I'll wager."

"Ignorant woman." He chuckled and nudged Comanche John. "Reckon she ain't ever heered of Marlowe. Tree of gold, and all that. She ain't up on poetry like we be, John."

"She probably thinks Marlowe's a bartender."

"Faro dealer!"

And they chuckled and nudged each other all over again.

"You're hiding something away from me, Mr. Browers." She walked around to look in his eyes. "You went and found something, or you wouldn't be good-spirited, in the state you're in. Let me feel your underwear. Wet to the skin. You'll get the horse croup, and I'll have to sit up and take care o' you."

"I'm wet, too," said John.

"Well, that may be, but you ain't my worry. Heaven knows, one dirty, no-account man is enough. But wait thar, the both of ye, and I'll fix ye a tonic."

The tonic consisted of hot water and brown sugar strongly fortified by alcohol. It took John's breath away, cold and hungry as he was.

He said, "Why, Mrs. Browers, you put *whisky* in this!"

"Don't be so aghast. I heered you brag to the boys about trading likker to the Injuns up in Canady. And I got nothing against a drop or two for medicine. Brought that quart of old Rough and Ready all the way from Kansas."

They fanned with a blanket, and coaxed the fire to a blaze. After supper it started to rain again.

McFadden came around and said, "What we ought to do is pack up and drive all night, get this stuff under cover in the wagons; otherwise every pack will weigh a ton, and we'll be four days getting there."

Buffalo rejected it. He appraised the black sky. "Rain'll quit." There was no evidence of that. "We'll chop brush. Get some big lean-tos made. Shed the rain. I'll not trust those horses on slippery gumbo, some of it around cut-banks thirty foot high. I say we better camp here until it dries off."

McFadden and Vanderhoff began to protest, but Buffalo outbellowed them. "I say this can't last; we'll either get a dry-up or a freeze."

His wife said, "You serious, Mr. Browers?"

He said in a low voice: "O' course. We're going back

after that gold. John, me, some of us. The pack train'll have to wait."

"We got no claim on that treasure."

"Yes, we have. We be the ones that put callouses on our hands whilst they rode around and played monte and got themselves roaring full of chokecherry cordial. And never got paid for our work, either. They never intended to pay for it."

John said, "Share and share alike's my motto."

"There, you hear that? Share and share alike—that's Christian. We'll get Chadwaller and Billy Harum. And Van, I guess. Let's see, with John and me, and McCormick from the other camp, that'll make six."

"Seven," she said. "You're not counting me out, Mr. Browers. I don't trust men when they get around gold, and I'll not have you hogging more'n your share."

Vanderhoff had constructed a rude shelter by fastening buffalo hides to the broad low branch of a cottonwood tree, and slanting it back in the direction of the wind. With a fire reflecting inside, it was quite warm, and there they gathered for their powwow while other men, near the main fire, worked on a brush lean-to.

"This is gold," John said, and dropped the heavy bag among them.

It struck the earth with a solid, rattly, jingly sound, and it had the intended effect. No one even brought up the subject of danger when the plans were laid for recovering more of it. Each one had an idea, and of these Vanderhoff's was the boldest. He wanted to ride back to Brule that very night, creep aboard the big boat, float it downstream, and use it for recovering the treasure, after which they need merely keep going with the current until a safe landing could be made, and there wait for packhorses.

Browers spoke against it. Robel, he said, would be sure to have a sentry out, and the boat's absence would be immediately detected.

It was Prudence who came forth with the most workable plan. "They waited till we was gone," she said. "They want to get the yaller stuff easy, and not start a ruckus, so they'll wait another day if they have to. Now, Nellie Huss is feeling poorly, I hear, and I've just tooken to worrying about her. So I'll go back and see how she fares, and long as I'm in camp they'll lie low, and you can get your licks in. And mind, no more than your fair share."

"Thar's a woman for ye!" said John. "Browers, you better keep close watch of that woman, or somebody with a real appreciation of brains, beauty, and venison stew will kidnap her. Your idee is first rate. Now, I'd like to get word to Billy McCormick. Want him out. Him and Mary Bird. Yes, and that poor, beat-down Huss woman, too. Robel and that crowd will go on the kill like a band of mad wolves if they ever found out we skun 'em out of the gold."

"Hearken a minute!" Billy Harum was up, trying to see over the campfire.

"Hear something?" Buffalo asked.

He shook his head, "Not me, but *they* did." He pointed toward the other fire, where the men had stopped working to look at something in the dark toward the river.

"What was it?" Buffalo called to McFadden.

"*I* saw nothing, it was Beans."

It turned out that Beans had been hobbling horses, and that one of them, Old Smoke, acted the way he always did when Eva was around. Smoke had once been teamed with Eva, but she proved too light for him in the hill country, and Harum had swapped her to Gilmartin, who had in turn swapped with Spotsy Huss.

The men got up and poked around through the wet brush along the river without picking up a track until Chadwaller started to yell: "This is all foolishness. That dog o' mine is the best barker in the territory. Not even a ghostly spirit could sneak around with *that* dog around. Especially Spotsy. Hates Spotsy. Bit him once."

Browers said: "Spotsy bit him? I wouldn't want Spotsy to bite me, I'd git hyderphoby for sure," and they all hee-hawed, and said Browers was the wit of the evening, and then they went back to complete their plans. Afterward they sat around, saying how smart they'd be with their share of the money when they got it; not go off hog-wild, spending it on a lot of foolish truck, but just invest it in something good and solid, and go on living as they always had, except a whole lot better.

At dawn, a grayness with rain, Prudence left, riding a big dapple horse, astraddle like a man, with an oilskin poncho over her head. The men finished breakfast, put some finishing touches to the camp, and began to catch their horses. Vanderhoff then came puffing up from the river with word that Chadwaller's dog had been discovered, drowned.

"Can't drown a dog," John said.

"Dis von iss!"

They all hurried down to see. The animal had been struck across the base of the skull, and afterward wedged head downward between two driftlogs.

John said: "Why, it does look like Beans was right. I believe we had a visitor last night."

They hunted the shore for a strange set of tracks, but there were so many tracks nobody could be sure.

Harum said: "That was a mean dog. Had a notion to kill him myself, plenty of times. Somebody right here in camp did it, I'll wager, on the sly, of course, so as not to make Chadwaller hostile."

Buffalo Browers was somewhat reassured, but he still went around muttering, "I tell you, if that Spotsy Huss eavesdropped on us, and if anything happens to my woman on account of it, the country between here and Canady ain't big enough but what I'll find him."

John broke it up, bellowing: "Saddle and ride! It's too late to do anything about it, anyhow. Prudence is well on toward Brule, and if we got spied, why, we'll just have to take our medicine. Saddle and ride! I want to locate that tree of gold before night sets in, because from the looks of things it'll be a black one."

The rest of the camp knew something was brewing, and they all stood watching and talking among themselves as Comanche John, Vanderhoff, Harum, Chadwaller, and Browers left, riding in that order, single file, back along the pack-horse trail.

It remained drizzly and cold until midday, when the rain stopped, and then it was just cold.

"Freeze tonight," Harum said.

"Too cloudy," answered Chadwaller.

The mud was slick and treacherous along the clay hills, and on the bottoms the brush was beaded with moisture which showered down at the slightest touch. Toward evening the sun came palely out, but there was no warmth in it. It sank into a cloud bank, and a long twilight set in.

They followed the back-country coulees around Brule, came down to the river, stripped their clothes, crossed, and dressed on the far bank. By that time it was so dark Comanche John had difficulty in finding Garrick's hidden skiff.

"I'll take this," he said. "You follow along on shore."

They dragged it to the water. John concealed his horse and got into the skiff. He said in a hushed voice to Buffalo: "Go up easy. Might be a sentry. If thar is, don't let him get word back to the Brule."

"How'll we stop him?"

"Bullet will stop him."

"I don't like that," Browers whispered. "I don't want it

168

to be us that fires the first shot."

"Ask Garrick who fired the first shot."

The skiff, tugged by the current, swung about; it traveled swiftly, and he was alone on the dark, silent river.

CHAPTER TWENTY-FOUR

Prudence, by hard traveling, reached the camp at Brule when it was still daylight. Her first glance told her that some of those card-playing varmints were still yonder, loafing around their lean-tos, shiftless as ever, and she could see that Nellie Huss had hung out a few pieces of wash.

Spotsy came out, and drew up short on seeing her.

"How's Nellie?" Prudence asked him.

"Oh, tolerable."

"I heard not. I heard she was poorly."

"What you come back for?"

"Because I chose, if it's any of your concern. Now hold that bridle while I git off. And turn your head the other way. I may ride astraddle, but I'm letting no man see my petticoat."

She got down, a bit stiffly, and straightened her clothing. While about it, she had a long look at the uphill lean-tos where men had straggled out to watch. There were Tom Claus and Dave and Sellers, and that worthless loudmouth they called Pete Limberlegs, who was supposed to be the camp hunter but scarcely ever brought in a carcass that a person could cook short of a two-day boiling; but she saw nothing of Gar Robel.

She said to Spotsy, "Take that animal out and hobble him, and mind you don't let him stray, because he's off'n

Mr. Browers's lead team."

Nellie and Mary Bird were both watching from the skin-draped door, Nellie peaked and scared, but Mary with the same somber eyes she always had. It was aggravating, being around an Injun, the quiet, dark way of their eyes, thinking but never saying, and never laughing at the same things that a human being laughed at.

"I see you're up and around," she said to Nellie.

"Yes'm." Nellie had a whipped look. She was pale, and she kept biting her underlip, and looking beyond Prudence at her husband, who was leading the horse off. "I just et something that didn't agree."

Prudence grunted. She blamed Spotsy for the woman's abandonment in the rain-drenched camp, and would have welcomed a chance to whop him again. "Whar's Robel?"

"I don't know!"

"Now, what's the pint of saying it like that? Has that timberwolf been bullyragging you?"

"He hasn't said a word—except to compliment me on the supper I cooked."

"All right, Nell. I'm sorry. I didn't like leaving you behind, and when I heard you were sick, why, I had to come; but, seeing it was a false alarm, I'll pull out again."

She spoke in a loud voice because that hawk-faced cutthroat, Wally Claven, was ambling that way with his ears perked.

Nellie said, "You want your horse back?"

"Ye mean start back now, without supper? What's got into you? No, I'll stay until tomorrow, and see if I can help. You don't look too spry."

"Mary can help."

"*I'll* help!" Prudence said, and that was the end of it.

It was twilight by that time, and Prudence started a fire in the outside cookoven. Robel then made his appearance, walking in his bull-moose manner, his pants sticking to the insides of his thighs from riding. He pretended to be surprised at seeing her, although she knew that his men had already informed him.

"Well, Mrs. Browers! And I thought you'd be over at the Sage, getting your wagons ready by this time."

"We'll make it tomorrow. I had to check up on Nellie."

That seemed to satisfy him, and supper went by without incident. Afterward she stood beside Billy McCormick for a few words.

"Everything's all right?" she asked.

"They come and go," he said, meaning Robel's men. "You should not be here. I doubt they'll go near the treasure while they know you are in the country."

"That's not necessary any more. John and my man went and found it."

He gave a low whistle. "Is that the truth?"

"Saw the proof with my own eyes. A bag of yellow gold, with the sack still slimy from the river. I came back hoping Robel would lie low for another day, and give our boys a chance to haul up a fair share of it."

"When will they try for it?"

"Should be there now. Five of 'em. My man, John, and three others—ones we can trust. You'd better get set to leave. You and Mary Bird. She'll leave if you do, and your next stop will be at a preacher's, or there'll be an Irishman with a split skull."

"It will be at the priest's," he whispered, patting her back. "It will, Prudence, honor of the Irish."

She cleaned the pans, and went to the lean-to. There, where none of the menfolk could see, she loaded a corncob pipe with cut plug, and lighted it from the grease dip. She puffed, keeping watch on Robel's men, with difficulty at first, and then more easily as the moon rose through misty clouds. Nellie Huss, crouched on a pallet, braided

171

her hair and kept staring at her.

"You look sick, Nellie. You look run down and haggard."

"I'm all right." Suddenly, excitement seemed to fill her. She crept across, cast a look around her to make sure no one could overhear, and whispered: "He *knows*. He knows what they're going to do!"

"Who knows what?"

"Robel. He knows what your men are fixing to do tonight. I don't know what it is myself, but *he* does!"

"How'd you find out?"

"Herb did."

"Who? Oh, Spotsy."

"He was at your camp, looking for a stray horse. He overheard."

"I'll bet he was looking for a stray horse! Robel sent that sneakin' man o' yours to keep tab on us, didn't he?" She started to get to her feet, with Nellie hanging on to keep her down.

"Please, don't! Robel will kill him if he finds out he told me. And maybe he'd kill me, too."

Prudence relented and said, "A'right, but if I had a man like that I'd drown him in the river." Her pipe had a bad taste. She knocked it out on the heel of her boot. "I suppose he knowed I was coming here, too."

"No, he didn't. That was as much of a surprise to him as anyone."

Prudence found her poncho, and put it on. She blew out the grease dip.

Nellie's whining voice came from the shadow, "What are you going to do?"

"I dunno. You stay put." She went outside, drawing the horse pistol. Nellie saw it against the moonlight, and began to weep. "And stop that howling. Anybody come here, asking about me, you tell 'em I'm asleep."

A candle was burning in one of Robel's shanties, but the poles had recently been covered with moss to keep out the winter, and it was no longer possible to tell by shadow movements how many were inside. She could hear someone riding, driving horses, and she thought that perhaps it was Spotsy. Something made her turn, to see Mary Bird standing very quietly in the shadow.

"Mary, what you doing thar?"

"Just watch."

"Where's Billy?"

"No savvy."

"Who's yonder in the wickiup?"

"Tom Claus."

"He the only one?"

Mary Bird nodded.

"Thunderation!"

She shouldn't have turned her horse over to Spotsy. If she asked for it now, he would suspect. She crossed the old camp area, now muddy, with all its grass tramped off. She looked at the moon, which was visible through clouds like curdled milk, and guessed by its distance above the horizon how long it had been since supper.

Robel and his bunch had had plenty of time to saddle and ride, but it would take them a while to get there, and to size up the situation when they *did* get there. It occurred to her that she didn't know where "there" was. She had never been down the river, and she had only the haziest notion of where the treasure was.

She reached the float, and was thankful when she saw that a skiff was still bobbing in the current, its oars already in the locks. The rope was wet and stiff, and she tore her fingernails on the knot. Feeling the float shake, she whirled around, knowing there was someone behind her. She tried to lift the horse pistol, but it was knocked out of her hand into the bushes near shore. Tom Claus, tall and unkempt, and laughing in her face with his liquor breath, grabbed her and held her helpless with a double hammerlock.

"No y' don't! I can still handle any *woman*. You got no shovel to hit me with tonight, Prudence. You got nobody to yell to. Not even to Gar. No, because he went. You know whar? To shoot the innards out o' that man o' yours."

She fought him. She was as strong as many men. She bent over, and tried to fling him over her back, into the river. He let go in time to save himself, drew a Navy, and aimed it at her.

"Maybe you think I wouldn't shoot a woman. That's whar you're wrong. I kilt a squaw one time. I did. Yes, I did, back on the Nawth Platte. I'll kill you, too. Don't want to." He laughed, doubling over and showing his dirty teeth. "No, all I want is for you to drink with me. You going to save yourself from bullet lead; you'll try a dipper of my chokecherry cordial!"

CHAPTER TWENTY-FIVE

THERE WAS NO MOON, but a slight glow from the sky brought out the river's features so that Comanche John could see the cottonwood saplings in time to swing around against the current and make the grapple fast to the sunken hull. Then, not wanting to proceed without help, he waited.

He waited for what seemed to be a long time, watching, straining his ears for a sound, cursing Browers as a bungler who probably could not remember the hiding place of the skiff. The sky had cleared somewhat, and he could see the rough eastern horizon backlighted by the moon. A moment later he glimpsed shadow movements on shore, and heard a guttural word from Browers. He freshened his chew, and breathed easier. They were doing something that took a long time, but finally John heard the creak of rowlocks, and the boat, breaking free of the shore shadows, came in view. Browers and Chadwaller were in it. They had left Harum and Vanderhoff to guard the shore.

"Here I be," John said.

"We see ye. Ye loom up plain as anything."

"Why, that could be good or bad. But I don't know as I like that jumpy Dutchman on shore in case Billy comes."

"Van's all right."

"I wish we'd brought timbers along."

"What for?"

"To set in that deck down below as a break to the current. It's bad down thar under the water. But we'll fetch the gold up. We'll fetch what we can carry, maybe *more'n* we can carry, and bury it along shore."

He helped to anchor the boat, then found the post that yesterday had guided him to the opening in the hull below.

"We'll have to take turn about in this cold water," John said. "I'll go first. We'll have to pull off some of her planks with the grapple, then use it for a hook to lift the gold. Sacks weigh upwards of twenty-five pound."

The air had warmed a little with a west wind, but it made the river seem colder. Naked, he went below with the grapple, set it, and came up to help Browers and Chadwaller with the rope. They tore one plank off, then another. The gold bags had packed themselves against a beam that served as a bulkhead. Standing to his armpits in water, John ducked repeatedly, hooking the bags on the grapple, while the other two pulled them up and dropped them in the other boat. There were nine sacks, after which, chilled, he let Chadwaller go below to explore for more.

A bar, as well as the grapple, was required to rip off the next section of deck. They found another cache of gold, four sacks, and loaded that; but further work netted them nothing.

"We got to go deeper!" Chadwaller said, coming up from the river. He was shivering so hard he shook the boat. "We got all there is on this upcast side. The rest is sunk deep, and how a man can dive and git *that* is a question. If you want my judgment, we'll have to rise the whole wreck and tow it to shore to git it."

Browers went below, came up with one more sack, and said that Chadwaller was right, that was the end of it. But John was not satisfied. He wanted to rip off more of the deck. He still had hopes that Harum and Vanderhoff, not yet chilled by the river, might be able to do it.

Chadwaller said: "Well, I'm cramped. I got to get out of here."

"Go back to shore, then. You and Buffalo."

"How about you?"

"I'll stay with the gold."

Browers said: "Find much more, and it'll sink the skiff. Anyhow, it would with you atop of it."

John spattered tobacco juice across the water, and said he wouldn't care to die in better company.

They pulled away, leaving him alone to lift and tug the heavy bags around into better positions to keep the boat balanced.

He was on one knee, with his head below the gunwale, when a gunshot rocked the air, seeming to come from all directions at once. He sat back at a crouch, going for his Navies before remembering that he had taken them off and stacked them with his powder flask on the stern ledge. He strapped them on, his eyes sweeping the shore. The explosion seemed to leave vacuum behind it, with no sound except its disappearing echoes. Then there was a vicious exchange, with the shore darkness laced by streaks of fire.

John lifted the anchor, and the boat began to drift in the current. A bullet struck the gunwale with a solid thud and, glancing, roared away. Another fanned his cheek. A third punched through the side, digging wet splinters. He dipped the oars and pulled for midstream.

He heard Bruce's voice: "There he goes! Gar, cover the narrows!"

Below him the river set in against a high bank. With one of Robel's men placed there, to risk passage would be suicide. He swung the boat toward the other shore. He was broadside, and a volley caught him. He lay on the bottom, seeking protection beneath the waterline. Bullets tore holes, showering him with splinters, and water geysered through a gap that had been torn below the waterline. John ripped one of the gold sacks with his bowie, spilling the yellow metal in the bilge, and calking the hole with buckskin. A slug tore through, stinging his arm. He looked for blood, but saw none. It had burned him, nothing more.

He cut more buckskin, working as the water in the bottom deepened, covering the gold sacks. The boat was now very low. He bailed with his hat and, when he dared, tried to get back to the oars. A bullet ripped the stern, and this time the leak was a big one. He tried to staunch it, but the planking was split, and the harder he tried to wedge buckskin into it the wider the gap became. He ripped out what he had inserted, and sat back to survey his predicament.

He had been drifting toward the narrows where Robel

would have guns waiting. He had no chance now of making the long pull across to the other shore. He felt the boat sinking under him, and he had barely time enough to lay down the oars and take off his guns. He went overboard with the guns and belts around his neck.

His memory of the river had not failed; there was gravel bottom under his boots. The river was chest-deep, and he waded toward shore with the boat's mooring rope in his hand. The moon was alternately bright and dim behind clouds. A brief interval of darkness helped. Repeatedly the current threatened to drag him off his feet. Then he was climbing, waist-deep, hip-deep, knee-deep, without a choice, directly to the part of the shore where the fighting had been centered.

He waded out on a narrow beach, half expecting to be met by the close volley that would finish him. Nothing happened. There was no shooting anywhere. All he could hear were the sucking sounds of his boots. Ahead of him was a dark undercut bank, some ten or twelve feet high, of dirt and washed-out roots topped by brush.

Strangely, no one had noticed him. Then he understood: all of them had been watching the boat, expecting it to drift around the bend. He still held the mooring line. He pulled it in, hand over hand.

Seller's voice said, "He's putting in to shore."

Black Dave whooped gleefully: "Why, that's damn' good. I been waiting for this."

Dave made a crashing, charging sound in the brush. John saw him atop the bank, directly above. He had his sawed-off shotgun aimed into the boat, which was then coming around in a slow arc.

"All right, Comanche, no use to hide in the bottom. Sit up and take it in the chest! Looky who it is—it's Black Dave! It's my turn tonight. I'm a-going to cut you to ribbons."

The gun roared, both barrels. Its double charge of buckshot cut a splashing riffle through water that half filled the skiff. John had dropped the rope. He held it beneath one jack boot, leaving both hands free.

"Ye overshot, Dave," he said in his easy voice. "I be hyar."

Dave saw him, and tried to retreat. John was slouched, with his hands dangling below the butts of his Navies. In that moment Dave realized that he had no chance except to stand and fight. He went for his guns, but John drew with his old sagging shoulder hitch. The Navies roared; one, two, right and left, and the bullets knocked Dave in a half-pivot. A convulsion of Dave's hand made him shoot once in the air, then he fell in a sitting-down position, with his feet overhanging the bank, slid, and ended in a crumpled heap at Comanche John's feet.

The others had heard Dave call out that he would cut John to ribbons, and they had heard the pound of explosions. They came crashing through the brush from up and down the stream to have a look at the body, and were met by a volley from Comanche John's guns. Men were down and men were retreating. John saw Claven, the hawk-faced man, and drilled him.

"Come and git it, boys," John roared, "I'm serving a late supper tonight, but my biscuits are still red hot. I'm Comanche John from Yuba Gulch. I sole my boots with scrap iron, and I drink water out o' the crick like a horse. I spend my summers killin' Yankees, and wintertime I den up in the rocks with the b'ars." He kicked gravel with his sodden boots, and whooped, "Ya-hoo, I'm a ring-tailed ripper from the Rawhide Mountains, and I ain't got long to stay, so step up and choose your holes, because this is my choice of a place to start a cemetery."

Robel shouted: "Bruce! Get over there. Pete, you too. By the Gawd, you run, I'll shoot you both between the shoulders." Then he called: "Claven! Claven, where are you?"

"He's hyar," John said, "and he ain't answering."

A volley from an unexpected quarter tore the gravel between John's boots, and sent him crawling to cover. Robel, from his place deep among the trees, was now getting organization back in the fight.

Comanche John secured the mooring rope and clambered up the bank, one hand in a clump of buckbrush overhead, his boots digging for purchase in a tangle of washed-out roots. He bellied over the edge. He saw gun flame, and fired back. He crawled on. His guns were empty. Working by feel in the dark, he reloaded the hot chambers.

The sounds of men crawling through dry cover told him that they were trying to get him from two sides. For the space of a quarter-minute there had not been a shot then guns roared in a sudden exchange, and men lunged through the brush. He heard the welcome shouts of Browers, Chadwaller, Billy Harum, and the big Dutchman, Vanderhoff.

Vanderhoff, above everyone else, was shouting at Nick Bruce, who was hiding and begging for mercy: "I don't care if you was my friend, you ambusher! Come out or I will chop mit my guns that log! Come out, swine, come out!"

CHAPTER TWENTY-SIX

ROBEL'S MEN, in trying to get at Comanche John, had stumbled against the nest of hell that Buffalo Browers had laid, and been routed. Now, as John listened, he could hear the firing and shouting of pursuit, first near the cut-banks, and then up one of the coulees. It would have been easy to suppose that Robel had been caught in the fusillade, but John did not fall into error. He knew Robel too well. Robel was wary of the trap; he was wary as an old ridge-running wolf.

John stood, holstered his Navies, and groped his way through willows, around spreading box elders, and across a steep wash. Every few yards he paused to listen. There would be two or three shots, and then silence. The stretches of silence became longer. Then, quite close, he heard a crackling in the bushes. It seemed to be someone moving toward the river.

"Gar!" he said.

The sound stopped. John moved to the shelter of a box-elder trunk. He listened again.

"Gar, here I be. I'm coming after ye."

He did not expect an answer, and it was a shock when one came, sounding so close.

"Come on!" said Robel.

John pulled off one boot, and tossed it. Landing, it sounded like a man's step. Robel fired, and Comanche John, with both guns ablaze, tried to get him in the darkness. The exchange was short but furious. Then there was quiet, and Robel's voice came from a new spot:

"You don't need to come for me, John. *I'm* coming for you. I'm coming to kill you."

John said, "Ay." He shifted his position, chewing and waiting. As the night grew very quiet, he could hear men talking near the cutbanks. He listened harder. His ears began playing tricks on him, and he heard movements where there was none. Far upstream he heard a splash. Suddenly suspicious, he started that way. He had forgotten about taking off his boot. It took several minutes, groping through the dark, to find it. He ran to the bank, looking down for the boat and its cargo of gold. It was gone. He hoped for a second that it had merely sunk, but the mooring rope was no longer there.

He cursed himself, then slid down the bank, with dirt showering over him, and ran along the river to a point where he could see for a mile downstream. The river was empty. He went the other way, around the first bend. There he found the boat, half filled with water, drifting, bumping on the gravel. The oars were gone, the gold was gone. He looked for the tracks of horses. Then his eyes noted the skid marks of the second skiff, the one Browers had taken ashore when he ran into the ambush. He knew then that Robel had transferred the gold and pulled upstream.

John ran along the bank. The weight of his boots made his legs ache. He wanted his horse, but he had left it far away, at Garrick's old camp. He kept going, thinking he would find saddlehorses concealed in each new clump of timber. He called to Browers, to Harum, to Chadwaller, but no one answered. He saw the boat briefly, the flash of oars in moonlight, and, at a hopeless distance, the bending, straightening form of Gar Robel.

It occurred to him that Robel and his men, passing, might have discovered his horse and taken him, but the gunpowder was patiently waiting at Garrick's camp. Robel, he decided, would head for the camp at Brule. He would find horses there, load the gold, and go on. But all that would require time.

John crossed the river again, this time taking off only his guns. He heard gunfire, one shot, then two more. It seemed to come from camp. He could not be sure. He rode at a gallop, a trot, a gallop again, until he pulled up at the edge of the camp. A fire had been built up, and he could hear the braying, wheezing voice of Tom Claus in song:

"She left her lousy miner,
Her miner, her miner;
She left her lousy miner
In Sac-ra-men-ti-o—"

Claus stopped his song abruptly, and stood leaning forward in an out-of-joint manner when John rode down on him.

"Whar's Robel?" John barked.

"How do I know?"

John looked around, "He war here!"

"He war *not* here!"

"You lie to me, Tom. You're no more use alive than dead."

Tom retreated in a rubber-legged manner. He was drunk or pretending to be drunk, John did not know which.

He cried defensively: "I got no control over Gar Robel. No man alive got control over Robel. No fairness in trying to hold me accountable."

"He war here, then!"

"He's gone someplace. He cleared out, he did."

"Him and a packhorse."

"Yeah."

But Claus was holding something back. John could tell that by his eyes, yellow in the firelight, and by the way he retreated. Tom wanted to get out of sight, and run.

"You been up to something. You done something you know I'd kill ye for."

"No, John. 'Pon my soul—"

"Whar be the women?"

"Mis' Huss yonder, sick. I think she's down with the shakes."

"Whar's Prudence?"

"She ain't here!"

John rode at him, and Claus retreated at the same speed. There was a ridiculous, double-jointed grace about the way he kept his feet and avoided obstructions without once taking his eyes off Comanche John. They were close to the lean-tos when Comanche heard a voice, muffled and strange:

"John!"

He wheeled the gunpowder a quarter around. "Hyar I be. Who is it?"

"John, John. That sure enough you, John?"

He recognized Prudence's voice. He saw her. She crawled on hands and knees from the brush back of the lean-tos. Her hair was strung down, and she seemed to be covered with blood.

She said: "John, I thought I was a goner. He held a gun on me. Forced likker down me. He hit me. He did. I got away, and must have passed out. I hid, and he couldn't find me."

Claus cried: "That's a dirty lie. That woman's enamored o' me, and she's been chasing me out o' sight of her husband ever since we left Yallerstone Landing, and she even come back looking for me tonight—"

"Claus, go for your guns!"

Claus dived to one side, and drew while rolling on the ground. He twisted, and came to his feet with both guns blazing. He was catlike and amazingly swift. His agility made Comanche John miss.

One of Claus's bullets went high, but the other scorched the gunpowder's rump. The horse pitched, and dumped Comanche John over its head. He lost his Navy but held the reins. He rolled to his feet, shifted the reins, and drew his other gun. A bullet spun Claus around. He got up and ran, fell, got up again, and stumbled and crashed through brush toward the river while Comanche John rode after him. Claus got hold of a plank and splashed into the water, where he immersed himself; only the hand which clung to the plank was visible. He came up for air, then dived again. John ran along the shore, firing at his head each time it appeared. At last the gun hammer fell with an empty snap, and he had to reload. John snorted at his foolishness, wasting time and bullets on small game like Tom Claus.

He went back, muttering, "Anyhow, he got a bath; but I'd hate to drink out of the river for a day or three."

He found Prudence hunting the brush for her horse pistol.

"Whar's Billy?" he asked.

She shook her head. She was still groggy from her battle with Dirty Tom and his chokecherry cordial.

"Where's Mary Bird?"

"Ain't she with Nellie?"

He rode to the lean-to. He swung down, shouting, "Mary!" and ripped open the skin-covered entrance. An odor of camphor oil struck his nostrils. "Mary!" Someone was stirring around, but the interior was utterly dark. "Mis' Huss? Mary there?"

She wailed: "I'm sick unto death, I am. You get away from here."

"Where is she?"

"*He* took her."

"Robel?"

"Yes."

"Where's Billy?"

"Kilt him."

"What!"

"Yes, he did. He kilt him, and my husband, too."

"You sure?"

"He swore he would if my man didn't help. My man run out. He fetched Billy, he did. So you *see,* he warn't no coward after all."

"Billy came and Robel kilt him?"

"Yes. I heard him shoot. Oh-h, I'm sickened unto death!"

He tried to learn more from her, but all she did was to repeat what she had told him. He turned, ready to ride, then he saw Prudence coming on the run, carrying the horse pistol.

"She says she's dying."

"Agin? She died on the Big Blue, Platte, and the Laramie. I never saw such a woman for dying."

John rode off at a gallop. He stopped just above camp to consider Robel's alternatives. Gar would not again cross the river, not with that load of gold. He would take either the hill trail or the one followed by Browers's pack train along the river. A hunch told him to follow the river. As he rode, he thought miserably of Billy McCormick. He had become fond of the young Irishman.

"Told him he was no match for Robel. Told him."

It was dark, and he almost overran a man in the trail. He pulled in so sharply the horse reared at a pivot. The man cried out, and he recognized the voice to be that of Billy McCormick.

"Billy! Ye be alive." He got down beside him.

"I'm all right, John. It's banged up, I am. I rode after him, and he ambushed me. Snake in the grass that he is, descended of the serpents that St. Patrick drove from Ireland. My horse threw me, and I think me arm and shoulder and neck are all broken."

"You stay quiet, lad," John said, feeling better now that he had found Billy not beyond mending. "I say a broken neck ain't so serious if you haven't got a rope tied around it." He made Billy as comfortable as he could, and got his boot back in the stirrup. "Stay put, now. Prudence will set that busted arm. Whar's Spotsy?"

"Hid out some place. Don't be rough on him, John. He

went to fetch me. On account of Mary. I'm depending on you, John—bring her back."

"I'll bring her—or send her. How much a start have they?"

"Half an hour."

"I ain't much on time, never having learnt to read it from a watch. How far do ye amble a horse in half an hour?"

"He's no farther than that coulee with the high cliff and the swallows' nests."

Comanche John said, "Ay," and left him. He galloped for half a mile, then eased to a steady trot. Best not to go in blind. Best to keep a wary eye when you started following Gar Robel, because that grizzly would turn and bite you.

The moon was high, and the clearings were very bright. He left the trail repeatedly to hunt the shadowy edges, and that delayed him. He picked his way carefully through the timber, and that slowed him, too. Several times he stopped to listen. Earth, twigs, and leaves, still soft from rain, muffled the horse's hoofs. He sang under his breath, but not loudly enough to keep him from hearing the scurry of nocturnal animals:

> "Co-man-che was a pious man
>   That come from County Pike,
> And the only motto that he had
>   Was share and share alike."

He stopped singing, and reined in, broadside in the narrow trail. Something had scurried, a rabbit or a pack-rat, *toward* him. He kept riding, listening. He heard a cry suddenly cut off, then there was silence again. That had been Mary Bird. There was danger, and she had tried to warn him.

He still rode, but carefully, at the barest jog. The timber played out. He found himself at the edge of a small clearing. It was ideal for ambush. Gar was the great one for laying an ambush. He stopped. He sat slouched and easy, his hearing sharpened for the slightest sound. A coyote howled, then howled again. Otherwise it was so quiet that his breathing, the breathing of the horse, and the little squeaks of saddle leather could be heard.

He spoke in his usual tone of voice, "Gar, I see ye thar!" and listened.

He heard the rustle of a startled movement across the clearing. There were other slight sounds, perhaps those of Robel changing his place of hiding, thinking, perhaps, that John really *had* seen him.

John chuckled, satisfied with the ruse. He dismounted. The horse moved with a crack of twigs, and a gun exploded with a white flash. The bullet tore past ten or fifteen feet to the right. Instinct brought his right-hand Navy out, but restrained the equally strong impulse to fire. He turned the horse, gave him a slap on the rump, and sent him a few bridle-dragging jumps into the undergrowth. Robel's gun whanged twice more.

John had used the diversion to move a quarter way around the clearing. He stopped behind a cottonwood that had been felled by lightning. He judged that Gar was now about fifty strides away.

He called: "You're jumpy. Trigger itchy. Know what that means? It means you're scairt."

He listened for Gar's response, either words or movement.

He went on talking: "We been bound for this, Gar. We been ever since ye skint out from Californy, robbing me, and leaving me prime for a hangman's rope. You figured you'd git me tonight. From ambush. But even from ambush ye didn't have the gumption. Went yellow inside, because ye knew, sure as fate, that ye were no match for me."

Robel laughed. He seemed very close, the sound carrying well through the night coolness.

"I have no fear of you. I'll fight you with guns, or with knives, or with my hands."

John was on one knee, only an eye and the brim of his hat showing above the trunk. "Then I got a proposition for ye, Gar. Before Browers and that bunch comes and gits ye from the two sides, I'll give ye your chance to fight me man to man. Put your guns up, and I'll put up mine. We'll stand together, and we'll walk in the moonlight together. Thar's a coyote yonder, howls every little bit. When he howls, that's our signal."

Robel was silent. Word of Browers being on his way had probably worried him.

"Taken!" he said, and laughed.

"You standing up now?" asked John.

"Yes."

"You walk into the moonlight and I'll walk in."

"*You*, and then me."

"I'll tell ye. You don't trust my honor, nor me your'n. We each got a cottonwood tree at the clearing. You sneak up behind yours, and me behind mine. Thar we'll show each other our empty hands. Long range. Nobody'll shoot a hand off at that range. Then we'll come out, both at the same time."

Robel thought about it, then said, "Taken!"

John crawled beneath the shattered log, and continued on hands and knees across the ground until he reached the cottonwood, where he slowly rose.

"All ready?" he called.

"Yes."

John thrust his hands from one side and peeped from the other. One of Robel's arms was in view from behind a tree about forty paces away.

"Other'n!" said John.

Now he could see both of Robel's arms.

"Ready?" asked Robel.

"Ay."

He edged into the open, careful to move at the same speed with which Robel moved. He took a step, then Robel took one; another, another. Now they were both in the full brilliance of the moon.

Robel's neck seemed unnaturally long. His buckskin jacket had been pulled down from his shoulders, and to the right, covering his right hand. Suddenly John realized that Gar had one of his smooth-bore shot-loaded pistols so concealed in his hand that all he needed to do was to lift it and fire.

John had no thought now of awaiting the coyote signal. He moved in a sudden pivot, almost as Dirty Tom had done shortly before. But John did not go to the ground. Instead he spun and leaped, hoping to make Robel shoot wildly, waste one barrel, and be put off balance a fatal fraction of time before he could aim the second. But even as he moved he knew that he had failed. He kept his feet and drew, and the roar of his Navies mingled with the roar of the double pistol.

He felt himself hit and knocked backward. The ground spun under him, and the sky and tree shadows veered above. His ears rang. He got half up, then dived as earth, bullet-torn, whipped over him. He was on one knee, with his Navies rocking first one hand and then the other. He fired blindly, in the direction of Robel's last gun flame.

He stood. Powder smoke was a veil between them. He walked through it, though he had no feeling in his body, no sensation of the ground under him. Even the explosions of his guns seemed far away. He kept going. He was like a man in a dream, walking.

190

He saw Robel, who was on one knee, his head bowed and weaving from side to side. Gar had his second double gun drawn. He saw Comanche John, and with a blind, gargantuan effort got to his feet. John hit him again with Navy lead. He pumped bullets into him, and Robel took them. With legs braced, Gar lifted the gun and, with all his effort, cocked it. He took a step forward, stumbled, pulled the trigger, and fell. The double charge of buckshot roared downward, cutting a furrow through dead leaves. Robel lay huge and out of joint, with legs spread and face pushed into the damp earth.

For a long while Comanche John looked at him. He could hear Mary Bird calling questions in Blackfoot, but he couldn't answer. He could only stand and look down at Gar Robel, and assure himself that he wouldn't get up —ever again.

Feeling was coming back into him now. He had taken buckshot in both legs and in one hip.

He answered: "Yes, gal! Yes! It's *me* that's alive."

"Billy? You savvy—Billy?"

"He's alive. We'll fetch him. Where are ye, gal? You're good with bandages, and I need ye. I'm bleeding some. He got me with buckshot."

He found her, on horseback, beneath a box-elder limb to which her hands were bound. He cut her loose, and by moonlight she bound his wounds with strips torn from her underskirt.

"Need hot water, moss. Maybe mud, maybe white man's salt."

"No, gal. You just bind 'em. See, the bleeding is less already. Just put tobacky on 'em, and gunpowder. Nothing like blackjack tobacky and gunpowder for bullet wounds. No, don't ye probe for that slug. It'll take that sawbones at Alder to git that one."

"Where Billy now?"

"Still worrying about him?" John got up and hobbled around. He looked at the packhorse laden with bags of gold, gave it a fond pat on the shoulder, and said: "Likely-looking horse. Good cargo, too. Better leave with it. If I stayed, it might be I got more'n my share, and I wouldn't want that. Wouldn't be fair to the others. Mary, you better come along. This is your chance to be the squaw of a country squire. You can carry my big cee-gars to me. Solid gold spittoon. All that truck."

She shook her head, whispering, "Indian girl want young white man."

"Yeah. Waal, *that* is the ignorance o' youth. You don't know no better. Prudence knows better, but thar she is with a man already. So I'll say goodbye here. You ride back along the trail. He's yonder, about a half-mile from camp. Busted arm. You mend him up. If they ask of me, tell 'em I drifted a piece. You tell 'em I'll see 'em one o' these days, after I been ee-lected to the congress of the Confederate States of America."

Daylight was coming, and it was raining again, but the black-whiskered man did not seem to mind. He rode, favoring right leg and hip, his hat over his eyes, with drop-lets of moisture forming along the brim and dripping on the pommel in front of him. And as he rode he sang in a tuneless voice, around his chew of tobacco:

> "Co-man-che John is a highwayman,
>   He hails from County Pike,
> And whenever he draws his Navies out
>   'Tis share and share alike."